Memory Jug

Patricia Martin

Hyperion Books for Children

New York

With thanks to Jerry Rongo, for his music history expertise.
With thanks to Darick Spriggs,
for ushering me into the computer era.
And with thanks to Ed Pratt, for his knowledge
of the Northcountry.

Printed in the United States of America.
FIRST EDITION
1 3 5 7 9 10 8 6 4 2

The text for this book is set in 13-point Adobe Garamond

Library of Congress Cataloging-in-Publication Data
Martin, Patricia (Patricia A.)
Memory jug / Patricia Martin.
p.   cm.
Summary: Having taken over the job of speaking for her younger sister Amaryllis when a family tragedy causes her to stop talking, Mack resents having to step aside when she is no longer needed as a mouthpiece.
ISBN 0-7868-0357-6
[1. Mutism, Elective—Fiction.   2. Sisters—Fiction.   3. Family problems—Fiction.]   I. Title.
PZ7.M364165Mg   1998
[Fic]—dc21   97-37489   CIP   AC

For Gregory and for Candyce
and for Bob

Chapter 1

The problem with a memory jug was that you had to be dead to get one. After you died, someone who loved you went through your things and he took what reminded him of you, like buttons or keys or parts of special toys. All these things got cemented onto a jug, and there you had it.

That was the story of a memory jug. Or so Harry told us, the first time he came to visit my mother, Maggie, with his memory jug and his heart in his hand.

"Harry is not something we need around this house, Maggie," I advised my mother.

"Oh?" When Maggie asked "Oh?" in that particular

1

tone, it was not a question. It was a statement. It said, "Advice to the lovelorn from my thirteen-year-old daughter is not something I need around this house." That particular "Oh?" never needed an answer.

So I answered right away, "That's right. Harry is an unnecessary encumbrance."

"And this is something you know from the depth of your vast experience?" asked Maggie.

"Yep."

Maggie mumbled "Uh-huh," and turned around deliberately, choosing to putter between her antique dolls and puzzles, rather than my opinions.

"Amaryllis agrees," I persisted.

"Uh-huh," Maggie mumbled again.

"I'm sure she did," Maggie said.

"In her own way, of course," I qualified Amaryllis's agreement. My sister, who was four years younger than I and very wise at the age of nine, didn't talk. She *could* talk, but she chose not to. Other people in the world needed to talk, but Amaryllis had me, the great Mack Humbel, to speak for her.

Our aunt Sydney, who lived close to us (too close, if you know what I mean) had her own opinion about Amaryllis.

"The child needs professional help," Aunt Sydney

would state, pushing her big, rectangular, black-framed glasses up from the edge of her pug nose and squinting her tiny eyes. She'd pull her short, pear-shaped self up tall and repeat, "*Professional* help!"

Aunt Sydney had her own opinion about everything, and it seemed that she always made sure her opinions were different from those of everybody else in the world.

After she was finished telling us what was wrong with Amaryllis, she would continue to inform my mother and me exactly what was wrong with each of us.

"I feel like I'm in college again!" my mom would laugh. "Your visits are like a class in psychology. Psych 101 with Professor Sydney Von Frankenstein!" she'd shout in a phony German accent and wave her arms, as if presenting her sister to the world. Then she'd shake Sydney by the shoulders and lean down to plant a big kiss on her forehead, to show her impatience and love at the same time. Just like she did with Amaryllis and me.

Aunt Sydney would huff and her eyes would glint like freshly washed blackberries, and then she would continue on with her opinion, as if there had been no interruption at all.

"As for Amaryllis, Maggie, she is repressing all that happened to her, and to you, five years ago. She's putting an emotional brick on it. And that emotional brick is stunting her emotional growth. How can she live a normal life if she doesn't communicate?

"And Mack is taking advantage of the situation! She has delusions of power and you're giving her too much responsibility! You're giving in to her demands. You are creating a monster!

"As for you, my dear sister, what kind of life is this? For the past five years you've been moving here, moving there. You cannot run from pain."

"That's enough, Sydney." Maggie would respond to the diatribe in a calm voice. "Number one"—Maggie counted on her fingers when she was listing things, when she was being firm—"there is no emotional brick in my Amaryllis. And Mack and I are drawing her out of her shell, slowly but surely. I know we are!

"Number two"—still finger counting—"my Mack is a master of organization. Why shouldn't we benefit from that? She takes good care of us.

"And number three, I am not running from pain. I simply am who I am."

Amaryllis nodded enthusiastically, circling Maggie's slender waist with her thin, pale arms.

I agreed. "It's true!"

Aunt Sydney would pat her salt-and-pepper hair, slicked back and tied at her neck in a tight knot, and say "Hmmmm!"

My mother and her sister were not alike. My mother was a swan. Aunt Sydney was a duck. Maggie sailed through life; Aunt Sydney waddled. Maggie sang; Aunt Sydney quacked.

But when Amaryllis had stopped talking and scared us with her silence, Aunt Sydney spent every minute in libraries and book stores searching out stuff for Maggie to read about kids who stopped talking. She filled our house with piles and stacks and cascades of books like *Juvenile Psychoses* and *When You Are Having Trouble with Your Little Ones*. Our aunt visited every doctor and nurse and psychologist and psychiatrist and anybody else who would listen to her story and try to help. She spent hours and days and weeks telling Maggie what they'd told her, because she knew how worried Maggie was.

And Maggie, in return, in the chill early morning mists, would get into a canoe she'd borrowed from a friend and canoe through the choppy waters of Lake George, all the way up to Turtle Island. There she'd pick bushels of wild blueberries, then canoe all the way back. By the time she paddled the canoe onto the little beach at our friend's cabin, her clothes would be full of stickers and her arms would be throbbing. But Maggie knew her sister loved blueberry pancakes so much, she could eat them every day. And thanks to Maggie, during blueberry season, she did.

When Amaryllis was four, she had quite a vocabulary for a kid her age. Everybody said so! And she loved the sound of her own voice so much that she chattered continuously—a squirrel in a pile of acorns.

That had been the best time of my life. That was the time I had a best friend, Michelle. She was skinny with skinny blond hair. She wore a big sunflower in it, all year-round. It wasn't a real sunflower. It was made of cloth, so it lasted forever and never wilted.

In all of third grade, Michelle's lowest mark was ninety-eight percent, and she spent her entire Christmas vacation teaching me the eight- and nine-times tables, which are by far the most difficult.

Michelle was definitely a best-friend kind of person.

And to prove it, she never once complained about how Amaryllis would follow on our heels wherever we go, chattering away.

In the summer, Michelle and I would sneak over the cedar post fence at Wallenhaupt's frog pond and catch frogs, always in fear that the mean and vicious old Mr.

Wallenhaupt would find us. It was said that he had a gun. Amaryllis would tag along and get stuck half off and half on the fence, and we'd have to take time to get her unstuck, looking over our shoulders for old Mr. Wallenhaupt. Michelle never complained. And if Amaryllis scraped her knee on the fence and wailed like a banshee, Michelle would just tickle her into laughter.

In the winter, early on Saturday mornings, we'd go to the flooded baseball field in back of Lake George High to skate. Michelle would bring a thermos of hot cocoa that her mother had fixed for us. Amaryllis would drink it all, then run after us as we skated. She'd get under our feet and trip us up and send us sliding on our backs into a snowbank. Michelle would just smile her quiet smile and giggle, gracefully rising onto her blades again. She'd circle around me as I struggled to get back up on the ice, slipping and sliding with none of the grace that was so natural to Michelle.

Others were not so kind and patient as Michelle.

"Does your baby sister always have to tag along?" whined Iris and Julia, two of my classmates.

I hung out with Iris and Julia only sometimes. That was back when I had the misconception that I needed people to hang around with. Iris and Julia played flute with me in band. They wore cherry lipgloss because their mothers wouldn't allow them to wear lipstick. Cherry lipgloss was as close as they could get, without getting in trouble.

Iris and Julia used their baby-sitting money and bought themselves bras about a hundred years before they needed them. And they spent from seven o'clock in the morning until ten minutes of eight in front of their bathroom mirrors, fixing their hair every morning. I know, because I overheard their mothers complaining about it in the Lake George Butcher Shop.

"Anybody who lets their baby sisters tag after them all the time is a sucker, Mack Humbel!" Iris and Julia would inform me. ALL THE TIME.

Although Iris and Julia each had the patience of a saint when fixing their hair, they were not so patient with other people or with other people's little sisters. Iris and Julia belonged to the popular girls who were, as a breed, short on patience. I never quite fit in with the popular girls.

The popular girls liked Michelle, but Michelle was not overly impressed with them. She was nice to them, but she was not their friend. Michelle was my friend, and she never showed any impatience and never, ever called

Amaryllis a baby.

Of course, Michelle moved away after third grade. I never saw her again. Everything went downhill from there.

When Amaryllis was four and a half, she stopped talking. Because of what happened. She woke up the morning after the thing happened and hasn't spoken since.

When Amaryllis was five, Aunt Sydney said, "There is something wrong with that child."

"She's just quiet," I told Aunt Sydney.

"Hmmmm," Aunt Sydney said, peering down her long nose.

When Amaryllis was six and still silent, Aunt Sydney said, "There is *definitely* something wrong with that child."

"She has me to talk for her," I told Aunt Sydney.

"My point exactly," she clucked at me.

At Amaryllis's seventh birthday party, to which only I and Maggie and Aunt Sydney were invited, Aunt Sydney reconfirmed her opinion. "That child is autistic!"

"Hey!" I shouted at my aunt. I put down my empty cake plate with a clatter.

Maggie took over. "Amaryllis had a traumatic experience. She responded to it by becoming silent. You know that we've taken her to doctor after doctor, Sydney! And look at all the reading I've done, and that you yourself have done. All the literature you brought me! I've come to the conclusion that Amaryllis simply likes her silence. Besides, with Mack as your mouthpiece, who needs to talk? Mack takes good care of her, don't you, sweetheart?" Maggie paused and smiled at me. She gently roughed my hair. Even though Maggie was tall, she never peered down her nose at me. Aunt Sydney always peered down her nose at me, even though she stood on her tiptoes and raised her chin up to do it.

Maggie continued to eat her cake. She said, between mouthfuls, "Amaryllis has simply become choosy as to whom she's going to speak with. She speaks with Mack. Doesn't she, Mack?" This was not so much a question as a plea for confirmation.

"Um, yes," I said. I cleared my throat. When I got nervous, I cleared my throat. "In her own way," I added in a whisper.

"Tsk." Aunt Sydney sucked her teeth at me.

"Tsk." I sucked my teeth right back.

"Now, now," Maggie warned us both.

Aunt Sydney said, "In my opinion, Amaryllis is not the only one here who needs professional help." She looked long and hard at me, and then she looked long and hard at Maggie. I didn't know which one of us she was inferring needed professional help. Maybe the both of us. Maybe all three.

"Maybe we could get a family rate," I suggested.

Amaryllis came into the kitchen, where Aunt Sydney and Maggie and I were having this conversation. She had chocolate birthday cake crumbs all over her white shirt, the boy's type of button-down shirt she preferred to wear. Double Fudge Chocolate Chip icing with rainbow sprinkles dotted her face. Some of the sprinkles sparkled in the long thin strands of her strawberry hair.

"Lord!" exclaimed Aunt Sydney.

Maggie grabbed the damp red dishrag from the kitchen sink. She dabbed at Amaryllis's face.

Amaryllis had Maggie's face, soft and delicate and even-featured. Her green eyes did not flash like Maggie's did. Instead, they glimmered, like emeralds. Her nose, like my mother's, was straight—a countess's nose. A queen's nose. I was the only one who had a curved-up ski-jump of a nose.

The three of us had red hair, but different shades of red. Maggie's was a strong color—amber mixed with copper. The red of Amaryllis's hair was delicate, a sunset over an autumn lake. I got stuck with the carrot-top color of hair, and to add insult to injury, I had loads of freckles to match. It seemed that Maggie and Amaryllis were the romantic portraits, and I was the cartoon.

"Any cake left over for seconds, Amaryllis?" I asked.

She smiled at me from deep within the remnants of chocolate and sprinkles.

"In my opinion—" began Aunt Sydney again.

"In my opinion—" I interrupted.

"Children of your age should have no opinion. That is my opinion," stated my aunt in her haughty manner.

"That's some attitude for a teacher!" I blurted. My mouth often talks faster than my brain can think.

Aunt Sydney turned red, then white and then red again. Her eyes glinted like freshly washed blueberries.

"Fastest mouth in the west," Maggie said, elbowing me hard, knocking me into my sister.

Amaryllis belched, loud and clear.

My opinion, exactly, I thought to myself.

Aunt Sydney missed Amaryllis's eighth birthday party. She had to take her class on an end-of-the-year field trip to the Museum of Natural History down in Albany.

"The dinosaurs can have their share of the suffering," I said. Amaryllis laughed her breath of a laugh. Maggie made a point of ignoring me.

This year Amaryllis turned nine, and Aunt Sydney couldn't say a word about her silence because Harry was there, bringing us his memory jug and his heart.

"At least he's good for something," I whispered to Amaryllis as we cleared the kitchen table of birthday plates. I wiped cake crumbs off the table, into the cup of my hand. I brushed the crumbs into the sink and watched as Maggie walked Harry into the living room. They sat smushed together in the middle of the couch, studying the memory jug.

"Good grief," I said.

Aunt Sydney stood beside me and folded her hands in front of her.

Amaryllis leaned against the kitchen doorway. She smiled a small smile.

"What do you mean by that smile, Amaryllis?" I asked her.

She looked over her shoulder at me. In the sunlight, her eyes were the color of spring moss. Their gold flecks glistened. She broadened her smile, and walked up to our bedroom. I heard the door close firmly behind her.

I stood in the doorway between the kitchen and the living room. Maggie leaned in close to Harry. Her hair hung like a satin drape, framing her face and shining in the lamplight. Harry's bald head shone in the lamplight, too. For once, he'd taken his blue baseball cap off. He should have left it on.

Harry was a big man. He was tall and solid as a stone wall. His eyes were blue and happy. He smiled almost all the time. How could anyone smile so much? I asked myself. Only an idiot would smile so much!

Harry had a fringe of light brown hair around the big bald spot on his head. He wore plaid shirts all the time, under his sweatshirts.

"Cotton plaids in summer, flannel plaids in winter," he explained. As if we cared.

Harry had many, many sweatshirts, all of the same color. It was the color of Adirondack pines.

"My sister in Lake George Village has a T-shirt and sweatshirt business. She silk-screens them. I get all the mistakes," Harry explained proudly.

So his shirts said things like Good Ol' Kale Goorge instead of Good Ol' Lake George, or they showed Indians that were upside down, or they had words printed backward, reading names like einreB, instead of Bernie. Reading Harry's sweatshirts was an experience.

Harry was a man whose interests had been all tied up in eighty-year-old fishing reels and minnow traps and the best way to build a sturdy boat dock. His entire life was a path from his tiny antique shop to his dock-building business, and back again. Until Maggie came along. Now his interests were all tied up in my mother.

I got tired of watching Harry and Maggie make goo-goo eyes at each other. I got tired of watching Aunt Sydney swishing at the dustballs that she felt she had to clean, even though she was just visiting.

I took a pink candle from the birthday cake. I licked the icing off its end and took it up to the bedroom I shared with my sister. Amaryllis was reading, lost in somebody else's words. I drew my Special Things Shoe Box out from its hiding place under the bed. I set the candle inside.

For a long time, I've kept a Special Things Shoe Box. It was getting fairly full. There was the small soft cloth with pinked edges that I used to clean my first flute. I smiled to myself. I was now on my third flute. It was sterling silver and would have cost a huge amount of money if we'd bought it new, but Maggie found it when she was buying some old stuff at a yard sale down in Saratoga, so we could afford it.

My box also had things from people I cared about, people that are here now, and people that were with me in the past. I have a petal from Michelle's sunflower. (I won't tell you how I got that.) And I have an old lipstick from Maggie—a color she used to wear but probably will never wear again. I have a fireman's medal, a golden circle on a maroon ribbon. That was my dad's.

As I pushed things here and there in my box with my fingertips, I thought of other people in the world who had definite things on which to depend. They knew what tomorrow would bring; they could count on it. They knew their front door today would be their front door tomorrow; their bedroom today would be their bedroom tomorrow. They knew their father would always be their father.

I had none of these things.

Since that night five years ago, I learned that I could depend on nothing. Because that was the night my father got killed, saving my life for me and Amaryllis's life for her. And trying to save our dog, Lorraine.

My father was a fireman. A really good one. He knew how to handle a fire—any fire. Except, I guess, the one that was burning down his own house.

He crashed into our burning house two times. The first time was to grab Amaryllis and me, leaping with us in his arms down a burning hallway, tearing through doors bright red with heat and flame.

The second time was to try to save Lorraine.

I had asked him to do that. And so had Amaryllis.

"Please, Daddy, save Lorraine! You're a fireman! You can do it! Oh, please!" we both cried, begging him with our hands pressed against each other in front of us, as if we were praying to God.

He went back into the burning house, for us. He never came out again.

Afterward, days afterward, when we were staying at Aunt Sydney's house, I overheard Maggie whispering in the living room, to a man who was our minister at that time.

"But he knew better! He was a great fireman! A hero! He knew better than to go back in," Maggie cried softly, wiping her tears with her sleeve.

The minister had answered her, "He did it out of love."

I remember that night of the fire, Maggie crying in the dark, standing in her pink bathrobe behind the fire-fighters' yellow tape, her face pale as the ashes that were floating on the cold night air.

"Don't go!" she had called to Daddy.

"Please, Daddy, please go!" Amaryllis and I had called to him.

I don't know if Amaryllis remembers. I never ask. I have my own silences, also. Just like Amaryllis.

I am a person who has to rely on feelings and omens; feelings and omens tell me what will happen next. That day of Amaryllis's party, I had a feeling about what tomorrow would bring. And I didn't think my feeling was necessarily a sign that good things were on their way.

We would have been safe if we'd stayed in the house down in Lake George Village. We hadn't known Harry then, and Aunt Sydney did not come to visit so much down in Lake George Village. Aunt Sydney had been busy at her school in Saratoga.

But staying in one house was not in the cards for us.

Maggie was a house sitter, along with being an antiques dealer. She would care for other people's houses while they were away, and at the same time she would find good homes for the antiques she was always buying. Maggie took up house-sitting when our house burned down. That autumn. That November five years ago.

When a person went away for a while, he'd call on Maggie. Then we'd pack up and move into that person's house, protecting it and caring for it. Maybe we'd stay almost a year, maybe for just three or four weeks, sometimes for five months. We'd seen a lot of different places, a lot of different styles. We'd fixed a lot of broken windows and painted a lot of chipped cupboards. Maggie put care into any job she took.

I found this lifestyle absolutely fine. Moving around was protective of us. Don't get involved, don't get hurt. That was my motto. I'd been in four different schools in the last five years. I knew a lot of people, but I didn't know any of them too well or too long. This was just dandy, in my opinion. Other people in life needed friends. Closeness just meant you'd get left behind, sooner or later. People always left.

In the beginning of that phase of our lives, I used to look for Michelle in every new school I'd entered. But then, I stopped. I guessed I was not the type of person cut out to keep anybody close.

Aunt Sydney disapproved of our moving-about lifestyle.

"What is wrong with you, Maggie Humbel? Moving here, moving there. You are loose upon the world! You, with two children! You have to at least provide them with a home base. This constant packing and moving, where can it bring you?"

"Homer's Cove?" I suggested. We had moved here to

Homer's Cove, which was a tiny town perched on the shore of Lake George, north of Lake George Village. We were house-sitting for a family that moved to Europe, temporarily.

"On business," said Maggie.

"Some business," I said, picturing myself sitting in a huge straw hat in an outdoor café in Paris, or skiing like a madman down the Swiss Alps, or stomping grapes in Italy, until my toes were purple.

"That's the kind of business I want! To send me off to Tibet, to ride a llama!"

"That's not the kind of llamas they have in Tibet, Mack," said Maggie.

"They have the Dalai Lama in Tibet, child. He's a holy man, a priest," taught my aunt.

"You mean, you can't ride him?" I asked.

"Maggie, that child . . ." began Aunt Sydney in a wheedling tone, bringing us back to the present conversation of why my mother didn't settle us down in one house.

"Mack, that's enough. Sydney, you have your own way of living. You are settled in a home you've been in for years and years. That's good for you. We are an unsettled family, by nature."

"Not by nature. By fire. By disaster. You're running from pain. You have to face pain to fight it."

"Nonsense, Sydney. It is simply who we are. We are nomads," Maggie said.

"Gypsies!" I offered.

"Don't interrupt, Mack," Aunt Sydney said.

"Gypsies," my mother used my word, standing up for me. "And being gypsies is fine for us."

"Familiarity breeds contempt, Aunt Sydney," I told her. Here's your hat, what's your hurry? is what I felt like telling her.

"Well, I can only say that Mother and Father must be spinning in their graves," said my aunt.

Other people in life loved to picture what dead people in the great beyond did in response to what living people on earth did. I thought dead people in the great beyond had other fish to fry.

But maybe I was wrong. Because I was sure somewhere, someone in his grave was spinning, or maybe it was the stars that were spinning, or the moon that was crying, or the sun that was fuming. I was doing all three. Because two days after my sister's ninth birthday party, Aunt Sydney called up and said, "Surprise! I'm moving in!"

Chapter 2

There are certain standards gypsies adhere to. As gypsies, Maggie and Amaryllis and I lived within change. But there was sameness within each change. The sameness was *us*. We were Maggie-Amaryllis-Mack, the *family*. The change was the *house*. We were like cuckoo birds, living in other people's nests. We took care of the other people's nests and made sure for the safety of the nests, but we only had to love *us*. We kept ourselves safe to ourselves. We were the sameness within change.

Aunt Sydney changed all that.

"We are going to personalize things around here," she

announced matter-of-factly as soon as she moved in.

The first thing Aunt Sydney did, on the first day that she moved in, was paint the bedroom my sister and I shared a vivid Pepto-Bismol pink. Its smell permeated our house.

The pink of our bedroom was the kind of pink that set your teeth on edge. It coated the walls the way Pepto-Bismol supposedly coated your stomach, in thick icky swabs of milky sweetness. Pink also dotted Aunt Sydney's gray overalls that she wore over her favorite gray turtleneck. Strands of pink-tipped hair swirled out of the knot coiled tightly at the back of her neck. She had pink splotches on the black army boots that she wore for "rough work," as she called it, and her fingertips were solid pink.

"You are done up in pink, Sydney," Maggie laughed.

"Cheap paint splatters, you know," said Aunt Sydney, casting the blame away.

"It's a poor workman that blames his tools." I quoted a quote that Aunt Sydney herself was forever saying.

"Excuse me?" she asked haughtily, standing on her toes to look down her nose at me.

Maggie told her, "Sydney, you can't go around painting other people's walls."

"Those people are not going to return to the states for

months and months. I'll simply repaint it to what it was, before they come back."

"Then why bother to paint it at all?"

"Tradition," said Aunt Sydney, going over the walls again with a roller and a vengeance. "You and I always had a pink bedroom. Don't you recall, Maggie?"

Maggie smiled softly and said gently, "I don't remember anything quite this pink."

"It was on sale, dear. Now that I've given up my teaching position, I have to watch those pennies."

Maggie shook her head and wandered out into the kitchen. I followed her.

"I suppose we're going to have to hear about her 'giving up her teaching position' forever! 'I did it for you, Maggie dear. For your poor emotionally disturbed family that needs professional help.'" I imitated Aunt Sydney with my most melodramatic voice, and gestures to match.

"Your aunt has never played the martyr, Miss. Mind your mouth."

Harry came over to welcome Sydney.

"Welcome to the homestead, Sydney," he said in his misplaced southern drawl. Harry was from Pigeon Forge, Tennessee. He should have stayed there. His quiet smile was becoming just a little too comfortable around us. The way he leaned against the fireplace mantel in this new living room, the way his eyes shone when he looked at Maggie—he was settling in.

"Good grief," I said to Amaryllis, who stood in the doorway of our bedroom, trying to take in all the pink. "Harry is definitely something we do not need in this house. And I know you think so, too, Amaryllis. Especially now, with Aunt Sydney living here! How much can a person take!" I whispered to her.

She gave me a hug, but she kept her eyes on the bedroom walls. She couldn't stop looking at all that pink. Then she grabbed me by the hand and tugged me through our new kitchen, which had a door to the cellar. The house was old and the cellar was creepy.

Amaryllis pulled me down the rickety wooden cellar steps. Huge shadows plastered themselves to the damp stone walls, like giant bats.

She led me over to a gray steel shelf. It was dimly lit by a single lightbulb dangling from the low ceiling, and by gray light seeping in through a dirty cellar window.

There were cardboard cartons lined up on the shelf. One of the boxes was filled with old bottles. They clinked and clanked against each other as Amaryllis rummaged through them.

"Maggie sure carts around a lot of old junk, from house to house!" I said. I brushed aside the cobwebs and the grit that had settled inside the box.

Amaryllis pulled out a bottle. It was a fine deep blue. I looked in the box. There were more deep blue bottles.

I shrugged my shoulders and said, "Okay. So?"

Amaryllis shoved four bottles into my hands and picked up a few more for herself. Then she ran back up the stairs, to the kitchen sink. I followed her, and we washed the bottles in warm sudsy water. I held a newly cleaned bottle up in front of the kitchen window.

"Hey, this is kind of pretty, y'know?" I said.

Amaryllis nodded and smiled, holding a blue bottle up in front of the sunlight that shone in through the window. The light streamed through the bottle, pushing the deep blue color of the glass onto her face. We stood at the kitchen sink, holding blue bottles into the air, washing ourselves in the cool pools of blue.

I felt letters raised on the bottle side. I looked closer. The letters spelled PEPTO-BISMOL.

"Pepto-Bismol?" I said, thinking of the Pepto-Bismol pink our bedroom walls had become. "You are brilliant, Amaryllis!"

We brought the bottles up to our new pink bedroom.

We set them on the windowsills. The light streamed through them and threw blue ribbons onto the pink, pink walls. The blue took the sweet ick away.

As the sun shifted, more rays of blue sailed across our room. The rays floated above us and beside us and below us and through us. We became part of a cobalt sky. We were clouds, Amaryllis and I, cumulus and soft and pale. We were a rainbow. I took Amaryllis's hand. We stood as close to each other as a rainbow's ribbons of color, and I felt I could breathe her breath for her. I felt the beat of her heart.

She looked at me and smiled. I grasped her hand in both of mine. I squeezed until my knuckles shone white.

"Will you talk to me, Amaryllis?" I whispered to her, desperately. "Please? Maggie thinks you talk to me. Please? I need to know you're okay in there. Amaryllis?"

She kept on smiling and squeezed my hand.

The sun shifted again, taking back most of the blue. But there were still enough puddles of it to help kill the pink.

"Good job, sister," I told my sister, giving up on trying to get her to talk. "How about a little mood music, for our new room?"

Amaryllis smiled.

I carefully pulled out my silver flute and played "Greensleeves."

"Oh, that sounds lovely, Mack. So haunting. And, girls! What an improvement on the color of the room! Good for you!" Maggie said from behind us. She and Harry stood side by side. They were holding hands. "Mack, Harry and I are going for a walk. Have you done your homework?"

I kept on playing but nodded my head vigorously up and down.

"Amaryllis, have you done your homework?" Maggie asked, ignoring my obvious stare.

Amaryllis nodded.

"Okay, you guys. See you in a while," said Maggie.

Harry tipped his worn blue baseball cap and smiled. In my opinion, his smile was as sickeningly sweet as the pink of the walls.

I stopped playing in the middle of a note. I put my flute down on the bed.

"Right," I said, not sweetly at all. I looked at my mother and said, "Please try to remember what we need and what we do not need in this house."

"I'll try, Mack," said Maggie. She smiled, as sweetly as Harry had, and she and Harry floated away. Into the sunset, so to speak.

The doorbell rang.

Sydney called, "I'm cleaning the paintbrushes. Will someone get that?"

When I opened the front door, an odd boy stood there. He had something strange in his hands and something strange on his face. I thought it might be a smile.

"You look vaguely familiar," I said to him, by way of a greeting.

"I'm in your homeroom. I'm in your math class. I'm in your art class. I'm in band with you. I'm Shadduck Fey," he said. He whined, like a weasel with a sore throat.

"Well, what do you want, Shadduck Fey?" I shifted from one foot to another. I looked him over.

Shadduck Fey was basically composed of bones and knobs. He was tall and had hair cut close to his head. It was as thin as a shadow across his scalp, except for one thick curl jutting out from his scalp, above his forehead. The curl looked stiff with grease or maybe hairspray. His eyes were the dull gray of the cement in Harry's memory jug. Shadduck Fey was colorless, actually, and he looked sideways at the world, as if looking head-on would have been too much for him to handle. His head was far too little for his body. He had skinny chicken legs sticking out of dirty chino shorts.

"A little chilly for shorts, isn't it?" I asked him.

He grinned at me. His teeth were tiny rodent teeth, and not too white. Then he shut his lips, and he looked toothless.

"So, what's that thing in your hands, Shadduck Fey?" He shoved the thing under my nose.

"I heard your mother bought antiques. It's a antique."

"Well, she's not going to buy that from you. That much I can guarantee. That much I can tell you right now."

"I don't want to sell it to her. I'm giving it to her. As a welcome to Homer's Cove."

"We don't need any welcome to Homer's Cove," I said. "And, besides, we've been here for weeks! It's too late for a welcome!" I stepped back, starting to close the door. I ran into a brick wall behind me. It was Aunt Sydney.

"Now, who's this nice young man, Mack? Is he a friend of yours?" Sydney's voice dripped with charm.

"No way!" I rolled my eyes in disgust, disdain, displeasure, and any other *dis-* word you could think of.

My aunt ignored me. "What is your name, dear?"

"Shadduck Fey," he whined.

"Shadduck, what is this interesting thing you're holding?"

"It's a welcome to Homer's Cove present," Shadduck Fey whined. "It's a camel inkwell. It's metal and it's old. Mr. Platte told me Mack's mother is a antiquer. So I brought her this."

He smiled his toothless smile.

"How lovely of you. Why, it's beautiful! Let's have a look at it."

Sydney took the inkwell from Shadduck's hands. Her fingers curled under it and her hands plummeted down. The camel was heavy.

"My!" she exclaimed.

"Camels are ugly," I said.

"How rude," Aunt Sydney said.

"Hyena're uglier," Shadduck Fey said.

You're uglier, I thought.

Amaryllis joined us at the door. She looked with interest at the camel. She took it from Aunt Sydney's hands. She smoothed it and petted it.

The camel sat with his legs folded beneath him. His S-curved neck held his head up high in a regal manner. A camel saddle with deep fringe was molded in the metal. He had a bit and rein stuck between his blubbery lips, and a glass inkwell stuck in a hole in his hump.

"Before the days of ballpoint pens, people used to use

pens that had to be dipped in ink. Everyone had inkwells. Some were real fancy. And in the schoolhouses, every desk had a hole in it. That was for inkwells. They looked like short glass jars. Some desks still have inkstains on them, from when careless children got too much ink on their pens. They dripped them all over," Aunt Sydney lectured us. She couldn't get the teacher out of her blood. She peered at me as if I were the careless student who dripped ink all over thousands of desks.

Shadduck Fey beamed on the doorstep. All this attention was going straight to his head. My aunt said to him, "I just know Mrs. Humbel will love this. Won't you come in for a visit, Shadduck?"

"I think I hear his mother calling him," I said.

"I guess I better go, then," Shadduck said. Did he actually believe that I heard his mother?

He backed down the front steps, down the path to the sidewalk.

"I do think that young man has a yen for you, Mack."

Good grief! I thought. Other people in the world suffer from yens. I have never had a yen. I wouldn't know a yen if I fell over one.

"I have no respect for people who suffer from yens," I told my aunt.

"Lord, you are something," my aunt told me. She took the camel from Amaryllis and set it on the fireplace mantel.

I sat down on the couch in front of the fireplace and looked at the ugly camel. I turned and looked at the memory jug, which Maggie had set in an all-too-prominent position in the front window. I thought, for the first time in my life, I am really stuck. The camel, the memory jug . . . Shadduck Fey, Harry Goodwell . . . a rock, a hard place!

Something was dripping off the white marble fireplace mantel. The something dripping was black. Very black. It came from under the camel. Either that camel had come to life and was peeing strange pee, or the inkwell was leaking ink.

I walked over to the mantel, inspecting the area around the camel. I bent and looked at the black puddle forming on the good, wood floor in front of the fireplace.

"Oh, Aunt Sydney," I called in my sweetest voice. "Oh, Aunt Sydney, guess what Shadduck Fey's charming gift is doing," I sang. Maybe things weren't going to be so ugly, after all.

Aunt Sydney stood in the doorway, her hands clamped onto her hips. She glared at the black drips hanging like melting icicles from the mantel. She glared at the black ink welling up on the pale floor.

"Now what have you done?" Her voice was as glaring as her eyes.

Maybe the ugliness wasn't going to go away that easily, after all.

When Maggie and Harry came back from their walk, Harry handed me a tiny bottle of the same blue as the ones on our bedroom windowsills.

"Found this for you, Mackie," he drawled.

"Gee. Another bottle. Thanks," I said. My ungraciousness embarrassed me. I slunk away to my room.

I held the bottle up to the light. It was slender and graceful and no bigger than a candle for a birthday cake. Its blue was the blue of a deep summer Adirondack sky. Tiny stars were embossed in the glass, across the middle of the bottle. It might have belonged to an elf, or a fairy.

Instead of setting it with the other bottles on the windowsills, I put it into my Special Things Shoe Box. It rolled, then rested against the pink candle I had put there, after Amaryllis's last birthday party. I studied the blue and the pink. I thought of Harry and of Amaryllis. In my box, I also had a broken barrette. It was lovely, even though it was broken. It was made of silver, and it had green-colored stones in it. It was Maggie's. She had broken the back off, trying to force it to hold too much of her thick red hair. She threw it out, but I had picked it out of the garbage and put it in my box. It had a strand of Maggie's hair, still attached. I thought of Maggie and of Aunt Sydney, even though there was nothing of hers in my box. I even had a little stack of old McDonald's paper napkins I had kept, from all the times Daddy had taken me to McDonald's.

Him and me, we used to go have Sunday breakfast there—just him and me. We were a pair, way back then, when I was a kid.

I thought of Shadduck Fey, too, and of the ugliness of camels and of hyenas.

I put the lid back on my Special Things Shoe Box and slid it way under my bed. Life in Homer's Cove was becoming complicated, and far too full of people.

Chapter 3

Homer's Cove is an old village sitting on the northwestern shore of Lake George. It was named for Lieutenant Homer P. Homer. Lieutenant Homer fought in the Revolutionary War. In the winter of 1775, Lieutenant Homer helped General Knox bring artillery down Lake George. They shipped it right down the lake, in the middle of the winter. Maybe they slid it. There was a huge snowstorm, and Homer P. Homer led them to safety, into the cove that became Homer's Cove. Lieutenant Homer saved the day.

People have forgotten that Homer's Cove is named after Homer P. Homer. I know only because Mr. Platte, the homeroom teacher for "Combined Seventh and

Eighth" (which is what they do in a school that has only about a hundred kids), told me to go down to the Homer's Cove dock and read the story that is on a bronze plaque on a boulder in the park by the dock. So I did.

Homer's Cove has one main street, which runs along the lake shore. The road's name was really Route 9N, but everybody calls it the Lake Shore Road. The Lake Shore Road has other little streets jutting out from it, streets like Stewart Avenue, where Turnips Antique Shop is, Fort Amherst Lane, where the Catholic church is, with its garden of stone statues. Horicon Avenue is the last street that jutted out of the Lake Shore Road.

Horicon Avenue is a big hill street, and the Homer's Cove School stands high on top of it. The school overlooks the village and the lake. The schoolhouse is brick and it has a tower with a clock that doesn't work. It had stopped at twenty minutes after five, about sixty years ago. Or so my homeroom teacher, Mr. Platte, told me.

"That clock stopped about sixty years ago. At that time, they didn't have the money to fix it. Then it just became a tradition, I guess," said Mr. Platte, scratching his bald head. Bald heads seemed to be a tradition of Homer's Cove, too, I thought

"Horicon Avenue is some big hill!" I said to Mr.

Platte, who turned out to be pretty decent, for a teacher. He was a beige person. He was all soft sand tones, his sparse hair, his eyes, his voice, his quiet laugh. His spectacles, which were framed in gold, were the only glinty things about him, although he had twinkly eyes and a twinkly smile. He had a little potbelly that stretched out the striped shirts he always wore. His ears were pointed, and he loved his blue suspenders. They had birds stitched on them, hawks and seagulls and mallards. He wore the suspenders day in and day out.

Mr. Platte was a person that a person could talk to. As long as a person kept it light. As long as a person kept her distance. Other people in the world needed to get serious in friendships. I knew better.

"I'd like to take a sleigh ride down Horicon hill after a big snowstorm!" I said.

"This town gets so quiet in the winter, you almost could," Mr. Platte said, laughing. Then he looked serious. "You know I'm joking, of course."

"Right," I said. Still, not a bad idea.

Mr. Platte chuckled. "If you had enough power behind that sled, you'd cross the Lake Shore Road and end up right on the lake!"

"Wow!"

"You know I'm joking, of course," he said again.

"Right."

Along the main street, the biggest store is the Grand Union. In the summer, when the tourists come, it stays open morning, noon, and night. In the autumn, Mr. Platte told me, when the leaf peepers come, it stays open some of the time. But in winter, the Grand Union is only open in the mornings.

"What are leaf peepers?" I asked, more interested in this new phrase than in the hours of the Grand Union. "Is that some kind of a bug? Is it some kind of a tree blight?" I asked.

"No. That's some kind of a tourist. They come down from Canada, like flocks of geese. They come up from Manhattan, like flocks of pigeons. They come to see the change of the leaves," Mr. Platte said.

"They don't have leaves in Canada? They don't have leaves in Manhattan?"

"Not like the leaves in the Adirondacks," said Mr. Platte. His chest swelled with pride, as if he personally hand painted all the Adirondack autumn leaves.

Mr. Platte became my town guide. He knows everything about Homer's Cove.

Next to the Grand Union is Finley's Fancy

Restaurant. A very tall blond man and a very short Asian woman run Finley's. They sweep their porch a lot and plant flowers along the sidewalk. There's a small sign on a spike, planted where their garden would be that summer. The sign reads BEWARE OF MAN-EATING PLANTS.

"Finley's strictly for the tourists," said Mr. Platte. "Kind of expensive."

"So, if you live in Homer's Cove, you don't go to Finley's Fancy Restaurant, but if you're just visiting Homer's Cove, you do?" I asked, trying to get a grip on this little town.

"Generally speaking," smiled Mr. Platte. "Sort of."

Next to Finley's is the Wigwam Shop, another tourist place. Then comes Mary Murphy's Old-fashioned Powder Puff Beauty and Neo-unisex Salon. That's a name that covered all bases. I had only seen Mrs. Murphy when she was driving her car. The car was black and very small. Mrs. Murphy was blond and very tall. Her hair was piled in ringlets on top of her head. The ringlets appeared to smash into the ceiling of her car, they were piled so high. Mrs. Murphy hunched forward over the steering wheel, and she looked like a witch on a broomstick, driving around. Her nose pointed the way, just as the sporty car's long hood pointed the way. She stared straight ahead, as if she were scared the road might change its mind and disappear at any moment.

Hurricane Hatty's Bar is next door, but they're seldom open.

"They open only when they feel like it. I don't know how they keep in business," said Mr. Platte, shaking his shiny head.

"Sounds like a mystery," I agreed.

Sheila's Diner came next, and everybody who lived in Homer's Cove had Sunday breakfast at Sheila's. It was the best diner in the world, and Sheila made grilled raisin toast that was two inches thick. She melted sweet butter on it and when you bit into it, you could suck in the warm butter along with plump, warm raisins. Sheila squeezed oranges for fresh juice, too. It had lots of little pulps floating around in it. Amaryllis used to call the pulps "little pupils." Before she stopped talking.

The first Sunday that Maggie took us for breakfast at Sheila's Diner, Sheila, who had curly hair the color of cinnamon and who was round as an apple pie, said, "You come by after school, girls, and have some monkey bread."

"What's that?" I asked. Amaryllis hunched forward, her face turned in rapt attention to Sheila, who was taking our order.

Sheila chuckled. "Come and see."

Both Sheila's Diner and monkey bread were popular topics in Homer's Cove. It seemed that people talked about them both, no matter where I was.

The second week I was in Homer's Cove school, Mr. Platte, who was standing in the hallway talking to a very tall girl and a very short girl, called, "Mack!" and waved me over. He said, "Want you to meet Miss Poppy Brioche, Miss Daisy Brioche. They're the daughters of Sheila's sister." Here, Mr. Platte spoke solemnly. "Sheila's late sister, that is. Their mom passed away years ago. They live with Sheila."

His voice came back to normal, and he asked me, "You're in band, aren't you, Mack? They're in band, too!" Mr. Platte appeared overjoyed with this news.

The very tall girl and the very short girl both stood looking at me and grinning like fools. The very tall one held her head tilted to one side, so her left ear was almost on her left shoulder. She seemed to be trying to get a different perspective of things.

I could think of nothing to say but "Are you really sisters?"

They nodded their heads like blossoms in the wind and grinned.

I stopped myself from asking how one mother could give birth to two vastly different kids. Poppy, the tall one, was big all over, although she wasn't fat, and had short hair that looked like a rototiller had run through it, and thick, thick glasses. She wore sturdy hiking boots and farmer overalls. Poppy was a clunky person.

Daisy, the little one, had hair done up in intricate braidwork. She also had glasses, but they were dainty, with thin pink frames. Gold barrettes were scattered around in her hair, and she wore a dress and tiny girly shoes. Daisy was an unclunky person.

"These two can tell you about monkey bread," said Mr. Platte.

"Yum!" said the big one, Poppy.

"You going to Aunt Sheila's after school?" asked the little one, twirling her braids. "We'll teach you how to eat monkey bread."

"Yeah," said Poppy. The sweet smell of strawberry gum gushed from her mouth.

"I think I can probably figure out how to eat bread all on my own," I said drolly.

Poppy and Daisy looked surprised at my response. What did they want, an immediate best friend? They had things to learn about Mack Humbel!

Mr. Platte chimed in, "Go give it a try, Mack."

"I've got to help Maggie move some furniture. Maybe after that, I'll get Amaryllis to go with me for some monkey bread," I told Mr. Platte.

"Who's Maggie?" asked Mr. Platte.

"My mother," I said.

"You call your mother Maggie?" Daisy asked.

"That's her name," I said, turning just a little bit toward her. My own unfriendliness embarrassed me, but one has to protect oneself. That much I had learned in life.

"Oh," said Daisy Brioche.

"Hmmmm," said Mr. Platte.

Poppy just grinned and tilted her head.

Continuing on our tour down the main street of Homer's Cove, the library sits next to Sheila's. The librarian, Miss Marmalyde, is Sheila's other sister, the one that is still alive. She is as round as Sheila. She has hair the color of a brass doorknob, and as stiff and shiny. The calm of Ms. Marmalyde made a person feel that she had been born and raised within the bookstacks that lined the back room of the small library. Ms. Marmalyde is the ultimate ideal of a librarian.

After the library is a park, Veterans Park, then Ben and Jerry's, which so far has been rarely open.

"You wait till summer. They never close," said Mr. Platte.

Across the street from Ben and Jerry's is Cobb's Hardware. Cobb is tall. He has white, white skin and black, black hair, and a grimace that he wears all the time. He looks like Marley's Ghost, out of Dickens's *Christmas Carol*. He doesn't find lots of words necessary. Things that other people say in fifty words, Cobb says in five. (Except when he talks about fishing.) But he likes to make sure you get the right thing in his hardware store, and he taught me what an eyebolt was.

Smiley's Deli comes next, where you can get FOOD GAS & WORMS. Mr. Smiley reads the paper behind the counter. He lets you tell him how much the things cost that you buy. Mr. Smiley never checks prices.

"What for?" he would ask.

"That's why he's never been robbed," said Mr. Platte.

Maggie always said, "There's a lot to be said for faith."

It looked like Mr. Platte and Mr. Smiley agreed with her. Carroll's Department Store sits next to Smiley's Deli. Carroll's has wooden floors and wooden and glass counters. When you walk in there, you feel like you just came out of a time tunnel and it's really a hundred years ago. The two ladies that run Carroll's are sisters. They both have hair the color of dustballs. They smell of dried roses, and their faces are lined. Their names are Mrs. Keith (who is large and never smiles) and Mrs. Francis (who is small and always smiles). Mr. Platte told me everybody in Homer's Cove has forgotten the sisters' real birth-given names. When they married long ago, people called them by their husband's first names. So the sister that married Keith Smallet was called Mrs. Keith, and the sister that married Francis Franke was called Mrs. Francis. Both sisters usually wear dark dresses with lace collars and cuffs and pearls on their earlobes. They speak in prim, subdued tones, and they clasp their hands in front of their waists.

Carroll's Department Store has shiny black leather shoes for old people, and it has Smith's "Work Pants for the Working Man," and it also has a counter filled with brightly colored plastic jewelry and sparkly fake diamond jewelry and necklaces and bracelets and ropes of fake emeralds and rubies and pearls. A person could stand in front of that particular counter for days and days, looking at all the color and the sparkles. A person could dip her hands into the boxes and piles of jewels and drip them from her fingers and her wrists.

I sometimes see Poppy Brioche and Daisy Brioche leaning over the counters, taking in all the color and the sparkles. I ignore them. Despite that, they grin and wave at me. Soon, they'll learn to ignore me, too. I'm certain.

The last building on the Lake Shore Road, except for the firehouse which is farther down, is the Country Store. The Country Store is sprawling and empty and for rent. Beside it, in the same building, is the SugarShack, a candy store that is not empty and is always busy.

"Every school in America has a candy store right down the street. I think it's a law," said Mr. Platte, laughing.

Our house in Homer's Cove sits on Maple Street, behind a white picket fence and under a very leafy tree. Maple Street is a little street that runs between Fort Amherst Lane and Horicon Avenue, behind Carroll's Department Store. Maple Street has no maple trees on it, only oak trees and ash trees and locust trees. In our yard, we have a big oak. So we have lots of squirrels. They scramble along the slate tiles of our roof. They sing in the early mornings, like Amaryllis used to sing. Chatter, chatter, burr.

When we first moved in, Maggie said in a reverent whisper, "This house is more than a hundred years old!"

Anything old and dusty impressed Maggie.

The house is gray with white shutters and a red door in front. It has a screened porch on the side. In the back of the backyard, there is a large, dilapidated red shed, and beside that is a dilapidated chicken coop. The chicken coop is as big as a small cottage. It has a slate roof of many shades of gray and pink, to match the roof of the house. A person could be very comfortable living inside the chicken coop, I thought to myself. Except it's a mess.

"The most beautiful chicken coop in the world," cried Maggie, when she first saw it. She clasped her hands together, as if in a prayer of thanks.

"What's so great about it?" I asked. "It's a mess!" Secretly, I pictured it all fixed up, for me. My own private chicken-coop home.

"It's beautiful!" exclaimed Maggie

"It's falling apart!" I reminded her.

"It's a Greek Revival Chicken Coop! And it's all ours!"

"For now," I reminded my mother.

"For now. Of course, for now," she agreed. Hesitatingly, I thought.

Inside, the kitchen ceiling is two stories high. The bedroom that I share with Amaryllis is upstairs. It has two outside windows in it, overlooking a garden, and two inside windows in it. The windows have shutters in them. When you open the shutters, you look down into the kitchen.

On the day we moved in, Maggie was excited. "Look, girls! You can shout your orders down to me in the kitchen! Amaryllis, wouldn't you like to shout your order down to me in the kitchen? 'Hey, Mom, toast me a muffin!'" Maggie sounded hopeful.

Amaryllis grinned from one ear to the other. She nodded her head with vigor, but she kept silent.

Maggie's bedroom is downstairs, at the foot of the staircase. The walls are full of cabbage roses and cherubs. There is lace at the windows and gold trim at the ceiling edges. "In my opinion, you got stuck with one ugly bedroom, Maggie," I said.

"In my opinion, it's splendid," Maggie said.

The living room is a square box with brown-and-white stripes on the wall and thick, soft overstuffed chairs and a couch to match. The living room, I could deal with.

There's a spare bedroom off the kitchen. It's tiny.

"Isn't this too tiny to live in?" I suggested to Aunt Sydney as she crammed her suitcases into the corners.

"Nonsense," she said. "All it needs is wise use of space."

All in all, the house is as comfortable to live in as Homer's Cove is.

"This is our best place so far, Maggie. And Amaryllis agrees. This won't be so bad. For a few months," I said.

"This will be wonderful!" Maggie agreed.

"This would be wonderful as a *permanent* home, if you ask me," Aunt Sydney said.

I looked at Maggie and Maggie looked at me. We both looked at Amaryllis. Amaryllis shrugged.

Aunt Sydney repeated with conviction, "A *permanent* home."

"Good grief," I said.

The day after Shadduck Fey dumped his ugly camel upon us, I saw him in homeroom. He sat way behind me, and he leaned over his desk, with his tongue hanging out. He wiggled his fingers at me and showed his tiny rodent teeth in a grin. I looked at him with what Aunt Sydney would call a look of utter disdain, and then I turned around and pretended he wasn't there.

After school, I met Amaryllis at our meeting place on the green circle of grass in front of the school, underneath the flag. It was our tradition, just weeks old but strong enough, to meet by the flagpole and to look down the hill, over the Lake Shore Road, out onto Lake George.

Mountains rose in rounded mounds on the other side of the lake, green against the blue Adirondack sky. The few boats on the lake were shiny white against the blue-gray of the water and the green of the mountains.

"Other people in life watch TV. I'll watch the lake for forever, instead," I told Amaryllis. She took a step closer to the lake, showing me that she agreed.

"I think Maggie's new old furniture can wait a little bit. Let's go try Sheila's monkey bread right now!" I suggested. Spring was giving me an appetite.

My sister nodded and grinned. Lugging my books and my flute, I lead the way down the wide driveway that the school buses used, for the kids that lived out in the hills. We bounced along, enjoying the clear air, the sweet June smell, the sparkle of Homer's Cove. It brought the word *jaunty* to mind.

"I am feeling downright jaunty today, Amaryllis," I said.

Until I looked down the sidewalk and saw Shadduck Fey standing there. He flipped a coin up and down in his hand. He looked directly at me, lurking and waiting.

When we got close to him, he said to me, "Wanna go to the movies?"

"Uh, no thanks," I said, trying to be polite.

"Why not?" he asked.

"Uh, I don't go to movies," I said, still trying.

"But I'll take you. It'll be with me!" he exclaimed.

"Nothing wrong with your ego," I said.

"My what?" he asked.

I steered Amaryllis off the path to Sheila's Diner, and in the direction of our house.

"Got to go home," I said.

"You mean you won't go to the movies with me?" he asked, as if he couldn't believe it. His thumb must have gone into shock, because it jerked up, flinging the coin he was still tossing straight up. It smashed him on the tip of his nose and ricocheted, hitting him in the center of his forehead, under his curl. His head jerked back and his hand flew up to his nose. He rubbed it and moaned. The coin fell to the ground and rolled, hitting the toe of my sneaker. It spun, then flattened itself on the sidewalk.

"There isn't even any movie theater in Homer's Cove," I reasoned with him.

"Oh yeah," he said. He stopped rubbing his nose and started on his forehead. "Well, how about the SugarShack for some candy? I'll buy!"

"Sorry. I gotta go home and help Maggie," I said. Helping one's mother is always a good excuse.

"How come you get to call your mother Maggie?" he asked.

"'Cause that's her name."

"Yeah, but . . ."

"Excuse us," I said.

"So you won't go out with me?"

"You're quick on the draw, aren't you, Shadduck?" I asked. Politeness had flown the coop.

"Oh, yeah? Well . . . well . . . oh yeah, Mack Humbel?" Shadduck shouted as he turned and stomped away.

I bent down and picked up the coin he had dropped and forgotten.

"Yep. Definitely bad news," I mumbled. I dropped the coin back onto the sidewalk, hoping that by leaving it behind, I was also leaving Shadduck Fey behind. This was one object definitely not going into my Special Things Shoe Box.

Amaryllis walked behind me, shuffling her feet. She hung her head.

"What's the matter?" I asked. "We'll get monkey bread another day. We've waited this long. We'll get it when we're left in peace, and it's just the two of us," I reassured her.

She ignored me, cramming her chin deeper into her

chest, staring at the sidewalk as she continued to drag her feet.

When we got home, she disappeared into our bedroom. I went into the kitchen in search of Maggie, Aunt Sydney, and the cookie jar. Not necessarily in that order.

"Your mother's out buying some antiques. Some old maps of Lake George, I think. One's enough, two's plenty," said Aunt Sydney, doling out the cookies as if they were made of diamonds.

"But I saw our truck out front," I said. Maggie drove a yellow pickup truck that had a green hood because when a tree fell on it during a windstorm at our house in Lake George Village, getting a hood in a matching yellow cost more money. The yellow truck with the green hood had orange rust stains grown along its doors, but it was our truck and well loved.

"Your mother went with Mr. Goodwell," said Aunt Sydney, smiling.

"I suppose you're happy about that," I said.

Before she could answer, Amaryllis appeared in the kitchen doorway, gripping a shoe box in both hands. Her face was bent over it, and when she lifted her head to look at us, her eyes were mournful. Amaryllis cared well for her goldfish and for her parakeets, when she had them. She was a good mother to her stuffed animals and to her dolls. When a doll broke so badly it could not be mended, or when a pet died, Amaryllis saw that it had a fitting burial.

From time to time, Amaryllis enjoyed putting on a grand funeral, even though none was required. At these times, a well-loved toy would receive the rites. Funerals seemed to fill a need in Amaryllis. Pomp and ceremony were good for a silent soul.

In the yard of each house we house-sat for was a cemetery, a Humbel Cemetery. I dug the graves, supervised the services, and played mournful tunes on my flute. My sister prepared the corpses and picked out our clothes.

I asked, "Who is it this time, Amaryllis?"

She held out the box to me. Inside was a blond Barbie.

She was missing her hands, half her hair, and a foot. She was old and decrepit.

"Poor Barbie!" I said.

"Put on your funeral clothes, Aunt Sydney," I said.

"What on earth for?" she asked.

"The funeral," I said.

"Lord!" she said. She patted her tightly drawn hair, shoved her glasses up her nose, and stalked to her room, muttering.

I put on the black dress that Amaryllis had laid out on the bed for me. It came from our dress-up box of old clothes Maggie was always dragging home. The dress fell over my sneakers. Amaryllis was done up in swatches of black lace and long black veils. She led us in a funeral procession to the backyard. We stood beneath a locust tree.

I played a short dirge on my flute. I made it up as I went along. Then I prayed, "We are gathered together for the funeral of poor Barbie, who has passed away due to . . . due to . . . missing parts. Good bless Barbie, the first unfortunate to be interred in this, our cemetery, here in Homer's Cove."

I paused, waiting for Aunt Sydney to say her part.

"Ahem!" I cued her.

"Huh? Oh! God bless us and Barbie," said Aunt Sydney.

I saw a movement from behind the picket fence that bordered our house. Shadduck Fey was crouched behind the fence, thinking he was invisible, believing that he couldn't be seen, even though the pickets in the fence were wide apart.

Good grief, I thought. Shadduck Fey and another funeral. Was this going to be life in Homer's Cove?

Chapter 4

When school got out each summer, I helped Maggie with her antiques. She went to people's homes and bought old stuff that they no longer wanted. Then the old stuff would sit in our house for either a short time, if she sold it to somebody right away, or a long time, if she decided she loved it and couldn't live without it.

Sometimes, she bought little things like teapots and silver spoons that looked like tiny shovels.

"To use in salt dishes, before there were such things as salt shakers," Maggie would explain.

"Ridiculous," I said.

Sometimes, she bought fancy china. She loved a certain type of little jar with a hole in the top.

"Hair receivers. Ladies would save the hair from their hairbrushes, and then make jewelry out of it," Maggie told me.

"Gross!" I said.

Maggie also had a penchant for a particular kind of chair, a small, fancy chair with a needlepoint seat and no arms. These chairs looked highly uncomfortable.

"Ballroom chairs were not made for comfort," Maggie told me. "They were made for girls to sit in for very short times, if at all, at dances. Hopefully, boys would ask them to dance, and they wouldn't sit at all. But if nobody asked them to dance, the young ladies would be so heartsick, sitting against the wall in the ballroom chairs, that they wouldn't notice if the chairs were comfortable or not. That's where the term *wallflower* comes from!" she added cheerfully.

"Good grief!"

"Well, that's the way it was a hundred years ago," said Maggie.

Sometimes, the rooms in our house were so stuffed with old furniture, we had to climb over and under things to get from one place to another.

"Isn't this exciting? Isn't everything beautiful?" Maggie would chirp, taking in the rows and piles of old stuff all over the house. "Life is a treasure-hunt!"

On the first morning of our first summer vacation in Homer's Cove, Maggie sang along with the robins and the brilliant eastern bluebirds that perched on branches lit by bars of lemony yellow sunlight. She sang with the squirrels scrambling about in the morning dew. She sang with breakfast for me and Amaryllis, bringing it up to our room.

"For Mack, three cheese ravioli! And for Amaryllis, her favorite strawberry shortcake! Breakfast fit for kings! For queens!" Maggie announced, displaying the tray with pride.

"Hold it," I said. "Since when do we get our favorite food for breakfast? You're the one who makes us eat Cream of Wheat! Oh, I know! We're moving furniture today, right?" I guessed.

Maggie laughed, and floated back down the stairs.

"Put on your work jeans, girls," she called.

"Yep. Moving furniture today," I decided, plowing into my ravioli. Strands of cheese pulled on my fork; I rolled my fork into them. Amaryllis wolfed down her strawberry shortcake, wriggling her toes under the sheet, grinning and rolling her eyes. She agreed.

Maggie bought three things from a very old lady she

knew when we lived down in Lake George Village. There was an old little couch that looked useless. Its wood was carved into bunches of grapes and weird leaves. When you sat in it, you didn't sink in even an inch. It was like sitting on a stone.

And it was too small to have more than two tiny people sit on it, but too big for one normal-sized person. "What a useless couch! What would you want with such a useless couch? And the upholstery is all rotted and wrecked! Why would you want such a rotted and wrecked useless couch, Maggie?" I demanded.

"It's a settee, and it's very old and very beautiful. It has history! That's why I want it," said Maggie, petting the thing as if it were a dog or a cat.

I heaved my shoulders in a huge sigh.

"Wait until you see the highboy," said Maggie, bouncing on her Keds over to this huge wooden thing.

"Huh?" I inquired.

The highboy was a tall chest of drawers. It stood on spindly legs that looked too skinny for it. As if it wasn't tall enough by itself, somebody had carved arches, like McDonald's arches, only in brown wood instead of yellow plastic. The arches sat on top of the highboy, making it even higher.

"We're not going to move this, are we?" I asked, sounding desperate. (Because I already knew the answer.)

"Of course we are."

"I should have known you had something like this up your sleeve, what with ravioli and strawberry shortcake in bed!" I said.

"Yes, you should have known," Maggie said and laughed.

Maggie and I were a team. We packed little things perfectly into boxes. We moved furniture, small and large, shifting together, knowing where to grip wooden legs or iron handles, knowing right at what angle to tilt a table to get it through a doorway. We were invincible! We didn't have trouble moving the settee out and into our pickup truck. And we didn't have trouble moving a little table with a fancy marble top. But the highboy was tall and clumsy and heavy. We took all the drawers out and put them on the sidewalk.

"We might have to come back for these. I don't think they'll all fit in the truck," said Maggie.

"Then you might have to come back for them," suggested the old lady. She hovered over our every move, wringing her hands.

"I've spent a lifetime with these dear things," she told

61

me. "That's why I'm selling them to your mother. I know she has appreciation for things with age," she said, looking fondly at Maggie.

Maggie turned from the truck bed, where she was shifting things around to make room for more things. She took the old lady's hand and squeezed it. Then she turned back to shifting and moving.

The old lady stood on the curb by our truck. She bit her bottom lip, in fear that something might get scratched.

"Maybe we'll take everything out and load just the highboy," suggested Maggie. She was stalling, circling the big chest of drawers, looking it up and down. Maggie was a master packer. She figured things out in her head, then she did them. This way, she didn't make mistakes. You wouldn't want to get stuck with a highboy half in and half out of your truck.

Somehow, we managed to get all the furniture into the back of the pickup. It was like a miracle. But I was used to miracles with Maggie. The highboy stuck way up in the truck, towering over everything else. We stuffed some of its drawers in between the furniture in the back of the truck and some in the cab of the truck. Whoever sat by the window of the truck would have to sit in a drawer. I figured I'd get to the truck first, to get the middle seat. Amaryllis could fit herself into a drawer much easier than I could.

Then Maggie asked me, "Would you mind riding in back, just to make sure things don't go flying? Please?"

"Can't Amaryllis do it?" All of a sudden, drawer-sitting didn't sound so bad. Hearing this, Amaryllis hopped into the cab of the truck in a flash, before anybody got any other ideas involving her.

"Hey!" I yelled. Amaryllis might have been quiet, but she sure was quick.

"It's only a short ride, dear."

"Eleven miles," I reminded her.

"I'll drive fast, to get it over with," Maggie said.

"How about driving slow, so I don't go flying out with the furniture?"

"Good idea," said Maggie, and off we went.

The old lady stood on the curb and waved, calling, "Don't drive too fast, now. Don't drive too slow, either."

Since the highboy was the last thing into the truck, it was the first thing out. We stood it on the sidewalk in front of the house. We didn't have a garage or a driveway.

"If you'd settle down, maybe you'd manage to have a driveway and a garage," Aunt Sydney nagged Maggie.

Aunt Sydney stood on the front doorstep, dust rags dripping from her hands, which were planted firmly on her hips. To show Maggie she didn't approve. To show Maggie she was not going to help in any way, shape, or form.

"You're absolutely right, Sydney," called Maggie. She smiled and whispered to me, "I'm not sure I understand her logic, but . . ." Maggie laughed. I did, too.

We set the settee and the little table into the living room. We put the settee in front of the couch and the table in front of the coffeetable. We categorized furniture, like cans of soup.

We put the drawers back into the highboy so we'd only have to make one trip into the house carrying stuff, not a hundred. We pulled and pushed and tugged at the chest of drawers. We put it down to rest and picked it up to move and put it down to rest again. We got up the porch steps to the front door.

"It won't fit through straight up," Maggie said.

We tilted it.

"It won't fit through on its side, either. It's too wide," I said.

"Tilt it at an angle," Maggie said.

We got it through a third of the way, so the top arches and the top two drawers were inside the house, and the bottom four drawers and the legs were stuck out onto the porch. The highboy stood at a sad angle, resting on its two side legs.

"Good grief!" I cried, collapsing in a heap on the top step.

"Lord," Aunt Sydney said, collapsing beside me, although she had done none of the pushing and pulling and tugging.

Amaryllis sighed. Maggie stood quietly and thought.

After a tiny rest, I got up and joined Maggie at the highboy. We tugged and we pulled and we pushed some more. The highboy had a mind of its own. It was not going to budge.

"I'm afraid it's stuck," Maggie said.

Hearing these words of defeat from her made me realize we were in a hopeless situation. This does not happen often with my mother.

"Well, what are you going to do?" asked Aunt Sydney in a curt, almost rude tone of voice.

"Nothing," Maggie shrugged.

"Nothing?" asked Aunt Sydney, an incredulous tone of voice replacing the rude one.

"Nothing," agreed Maggie, nodding her head with finality.

"You mean you're just going to leave this thing sticking halfway in the house and halfway out of the house," wailed Aunt Sydney.

"For now. Don't worry. We'll straighten it all out, in time," Maggie responded cheerfully. *She* was not worried.

"But . . . but . . . how can that be?" sputtered Aunt Sydney.

I said, "Don't underestimate us, Aunt Sydney!" I jumped up from the step and stepped over to Maggie. I put my arm around her shoulders.

"But . . . but . . ." Aunt Sydney continued to sputter, like an outboard motor on an old boat.

"Sydney, I'm not going to try anymore right now. We're frustrated, and we might end up wrecking the furniture or the doorway. We'll tackle it later. For now we'll just have to use the back door," explained Maggie with great patience. I can't figure out where Maggie gets all her patience.

Amaryllis had already started for the back of the house. I followed her.

"Hey, you ladies need some help! I can move this. Here, back up, move over, let a man handle things. Don't worry, I'm here to save your day!" I couldn't mistake the weasel voice of Shadduck Fey. I stopped in my tracks and ran back to the front steps.

Maggie said to him, "Thanks very much, Shadduck, but we'll manage." She planted herself directly between Shadduck and the highboy. She folded her arms in front of her, like a sentry guarding a palace, and stood rigid—an oak.

"Let him help," said Aunt Sydney, grabbing Maggie's arm and yanking her out from between Shadduck and the highboy.

"Go ahead, dear," she told Shadduck.

"Certainly. Now, all we have to do is move this a little this way, and move that a little that way, and . . ."

Creeeeek! Crunch! The door frame splintered, caving itself in around the huge chest of drawers. Shadduck stepped back and stared in disbelief.

Aunt Sydney gasped. "Lord!" she cried.

Maggie ran over and hugged the highboy, as if to ease its pain. "Oh, oh! It made it for a hundred years without a scratch—and now this! It's lodged tight! I don't know how we'll ever get it out!"

Shadduck cried, "It wasn't my fault! I didn't do it!"

"Did too, you nitwit!" I yelled. I punched him in the shoulder.

Shadduck yelped and pointed to Aunt Sydney. "You made me do it, you old prune!" and he turned and fled down the street.

Aunt Sydney reeled and grabbed her chest, as if she were going to have a heart attack. "I'm shocked! Shadduck Fey, I am shocked to the core of my existence!" she shouted after him.

Maggie steadied her sister. Then she ran over to the highboy, caressing it, murmuring and surveying the damage.

She called to me, "Mack, get the shower curtain. We'll cover this up, in case it rains."

"But how will we take showers?" asked Aunt Sydney.

"Very carefully," answered Maggie.

As I ran down the steps, Poppy and Daisy Brioche came running up the walk to our house. For the first time ever, neither one of them wore a smile. Their eyes were big and round. They held their arms up, bent at the elbow, their hands flying up and down like the wings of swallows.

Daisy screamed at me, "We saw what happened! We saw Shadduck Fey! Can we help?"

Poppy nodded her head. "Can we help!" she echoed, in a scream more than a question.

Before I could answer, I heard Aunt Sydney gush, "Oh, you dear girls, please, please."

They ran up to her and held her as she went through yet another collapse. They made all kinds of clucks and gasps, as if they were witnessing a death or some other horror.

Good grief, I yelled inside my mind. I turned and headed for the back of the house.

I ran into the big bathroom downstairs, the one that had the tub and shower. I ripped the shower curtain off its hooks.

"Even more people interfering with my family!" I told the bathtub, jamming the words out through clenched teeth.

"*Some* people in my family seem to like strangers more than they like *me*," I told the toilet.

"Well, let's see *strangers* get that highboy unstuck!" I told the sink.

I said to the towel rack, "There isn't a thing that's stuck that we cannot get unstuck, Maggie and me. We're a team! And *nobody* else is on this team! Because Maggie and I don't need anybody else!"

I ran back outside and around to the front of the house. As I jumped up the steps, I heard Aunt Sydney, who had calmed down to her usual self, say to Poppy and to Daisy and to Maggie and to anyone who would listen,

"Just fortunate it's not midwinter!" She spat the words out, one by one.

Poppy and Daisy Brioche huffed along with her, in agreement. Maggie paid no attention. Aunt Sydney picked up the rags she'd been using to dust, before we drove up with our furniture and our problems.

"Most very fortunate," she enunciated, nodding her head sharply once. She walked majestically around to the back of the house.

Daisy and Poppy Brioche kind of shuffled their feet and moped around, looking at the highboy and at Maggie and at me. We all three ignored them, me because ignoring people was what I did, Maggie because she was totally absorbed in the highboy, and the highboy because it was a piece of furniture.

Finally, they gave up, murmured a good-bye, and started to walk away.

Maggie came to and noticed they were leaving. She called, "Thank you so very much for your help, ladies. I really appreciate it." She gave them her Maggie smile, blew them a kiss, and won their hearts forever.

Daisy and Poppy cheered right up, grinned widely, giggled, and waved back. They skipped off down the sidewalk.

Good grief.

For days, the highboy was a part of the architecture of our house, with its head tucked inside and its rear exposed to the world. We used the kitchen door. When the night air crept in and made us chilly, Maggie handed out extra sweaters and made us hot tea with lemon and honey.

The third day of the highboy affair, it rained. Maggie tucked the highboy up tight in its shower curtain. We mopped the floor around the highboy, where the raindrops cascaded in.

Often, I'd come upon Maggie standing, with her hands tucked behind her into her belt, studying the highboy situation.

"Sure is a pretty piece," she'd say.

"Sure is," I agreed.

And then Harry came over.

"Why didn't you call me?" he asked.

"No emergency," Maggie shrugged, a shy pink smile on her lips.

Harry smiled his slow smile. He chuckled.

"You're some woman, Maggie-girl," he said.

Harry unstuck the highboy. First, he unhinged the door and took it off. Then he unnailed the doorframe and took that off. The tall chest of drawers slid through. He and Maggie carried it into the dining room and put it into the Things-with-Drawers section.

"Can I help?" I asked, attempting to elbow Harry away.

Harry didn't even notice my elbow; he said to me, "No, thanks, Mackie. Your mom and I got it. Stand aside. Don't want to squish you or anything," he said, laughing.

"Thanks, anyway, Mack," Maggie said. They swept blithely past me, easing the highboy through the house. They made it look as if it were made of tissue paper! Of feathers!

"I suppose you could carry it all by yourself, Harry," I said, in a mean tone. I felt left out.

"No, no, Mackie. I need your mom," he gushed. Both he and Maggie blushed.

"I need to puke," I said. Neither of them heard me.

Were my furniture-moving days over? I felt alone, with no team spirit and no team. They had been taken away from me.

By Harry.

Chapter 5

While Maggie and Harry settled the highboy into a good spot, where people wouldn't have to bang into it when trying to navigate the dining room, I wandered into my bedroom and got my flute. I wandered back out into the living room and sank into the couch. I played "Greensleeves" (I played "Greensleeves" a lot!).

Somebody once said, "Music hath charms to soothe the savage breast." I always thought it was "savage beast." I would have preferred "beast" to "breast," because it is less embarrassing to say. But you can't change history. Or quotes. I looked it up in one of my favorite books,

Famous Quotations, by John Bartlett. That's where I found out it was "breast," not "beast." I also found out it was William Congreve who said it. I have no idea who William Congreve was, but he lived from 1670 until 1729, and he must have been very smart. Because music—especially "Greensleeves"—does soothe things.

While I played, I looked at Shadduck Fey's camel. It still sat on the mantel, regarding the room. Its iron eyes were hooded, and they made him look pompous. He kept his hooded eyes open, watching me. That camel would have to go. Maybe we could arrange for a funeral for him.

Unfortunately, I was the only one in the household who felt that way about Shadduck Fey's camel. Everybody else seemed enchanted.

The camel studied me, as I studied Harry's memory jug, still in its place of honor on the living room windowsill. Amaryllis joined me on the couch. She reached behind us and took the memory jug off the windowsill. She put it into my lap. Together, we looked at it.

A memory jug was an ugly thing. Like a camel. When Harry first brought the jug over, it was dirty gray all over, an odd-shaped thing covered with other odd-shaped things, held together with lumpy cement.

Then Maggie washed it in the kitchen sink. She used sudsy water and her soft vegetable cleaning brush.

"I hope you throw that brush out when you're done. No telling where that jug has been," I advised Maggie.

"Thanks for your input, Mack," Maggie said, not paying the least attention to my advice.

Once the jug had been cleaned, the things in it gleamed and shone.

"That jug's about a hundred years old," Harry called to Amaryllis and me. He and Maggie were finally done fidgeting around with the highboy. They went to put on a pot of tea. Amaryllis and I continued to study the memory jug.

I guessed if the jug were about a hundred years old, the things in it were even older. There were lots of buttons. Whoever the memory jug was made for must have loved buttons! There were buttons of silver, with tiny golden leaves embedded in them. There were buttons of something smooth and opalescent that glistened in soft shades of pink and blue and pale gray.

"Mother-of-pearl," said Maggie. "The inside of shells," she said, running her fingertips gently over the shiny buttons. She had brought in a tray of teacups and the teapot and joined Amaryllis and me on the couch. Harry followed her in and sat in a chair that sat in a circle of antique footstools, waiting to find a home. He put one foot on a blue one, and another on a red one with purple fringe.

The memory jug had buttons of shiny black jet that glinted like tiny stars. A ring of sharp jet beads surrounded the mouth of the jug. A large clear-glass marble was set within the opening. It looked like a miniature galaxy of black stars orbiting a glass sun.

There were swirly blue, white, and orange marbles set into the jug, and a tiny pale-white china doll.

Harry told us, "That's Frozen Charlotte. She can't move anything. She's got no joints. She's frozen, forever. Poor Charlotte!"

The idea of Frozen Charlotte made me itch. I liked to move. Even when I sat in front of the TV or at my desk in school, I jiggled my foot or tapped my finger. Frozen Charlotte was an eternal prisoner of her joints.

There was a teensy blue jug, no bigger than my thumbnail, set in the jug, and the porcelain head of a cocker spaniel. Its glass eyes were amber. There were seashells and a tiny shield made of mother-of-pearl, with a golden *P* on it. Another shield had a golden *R* on it. Whoever's jug it was must have had the initials *P* and *R*. Maybe it meant Royal Person. Or Princess Rolanda! Maybe a gypsy princess!

There was a key and a crown made of jewels that looked like rubies. And there were eyes. Eyes and eyes stuck in the cement everywhere. Doll eyes, perpetually open and perpetually staring. No matter where you turned the jug, there was another eye looking at you. Staring eyes made me nervous. I didn't like the feeling of being watched. Even when I was upstairs in the bathroom, where the window looked out on nothing but trees and sky, and there were no houses with windows with possible peeping toms, I kept the curtain closed. I liked to be sealed in. You never know. You have to be prepared for any surprise—a low-flying helicopter with a curious pilot, a man on stilts. A person just never knows anymore!

Also on the memory jug there was a tiny lantern and a silver barrette and a tiny, tiny teakettle. There were so many tiny things, I wondered if the jug was made for a dead child.

Each time I looked at the jug, I saw something different in it.

After Harry left, after he'd put the highboy in "exactly the right spot" (as Maggie told him), after he'd "worked his magic" (as Maggie said to him) and gotten the dents out of the highboy by ironing it under a damp cloth

("How do you know these things?" Maggie gushed in a way highly uncharacteristic of her), after Harry had proven he was a magician and I was useless, Maggie said, "Isn't that jug something, girls? I love it!"

I looked up at her. "It's sad we didn't make one of these memory jugs for Daddy," I said.

"I know," she said. She took my hand and rubbed it. She nuzzled my ear with her nose. Her hair smelled like lilacs.

Amaryllis crawled into Maggie's lap even though she was too tall to sit in laps. Her legs dangled over, and she had to bend down to tuck her head into the curve of Maggie's neck.

"I know," Maggie said again, cradling Amaryllis, patting her.

Daddy and me and Maggie and Amaryllis, that's how it had been, so very long ago.

Daddy had taught at the Lake George High School. He was an English teacher, and everywhere he went, he carried a book. He even carried a book when he went to the food store, so he'd have something to read while he stood in line. But he seldom got to read it because he was always talking to people. Daddy loved to talk to people. More exactly, he loved to listen to them.

"People are so interesting! The stories I hear!" Daddy used to say. People, strangers, always ended up telling him their life stories. And he always had time to listen.

"If there isn't any time to listen to other people, what is there time for, anyway?" he would ask.

He was a volunteer fireman, too, and people would talk about having him for the firechief. He was a very good fireman.

"Too good. He's too sure of himself," Aunt Sydney always said before the fire that took my home and my Dad. After the fire, Aunt Sydney never said anything about Dad. Except, "I do miss him, Maggie."

"We all do, Sydney. We surely all do," Maggie would say.

Daddy used to come pick me up after school. That was when Amaryllis was too young for school; she'd be home with Maggie. Daddy and me, we'd go to Stewart's and get the paper. Once a week, on Wednesdays, we'd have an ice-cream cone. Daddy always got mint chocolate chip.

"Nothing like mint chocolate chip!" he always said.

Every Sunday after church, we'd go for a ride, the four of us. Daddy'd find us tickle bumps. That's when you're in the car, go up a hill real fast, crest the hill and then start down. Your body would come down, but your stomach would stay up, and you'd feel an intense tickle inside. We all loved tickle bumps—all four of us.

On Saturdays, Daddy and I and Amaryllis put the garbage in the back of the pickup truck, and we'd go to the dump. It was at the end of a very bumpy dirt road, and Daddy would sing "TO-DA-DUMP! TO-DA-DUMP!" all the way there. Daddy could be pretty corny at times.

Maggie had agreed. She'd ruffle his hair, just like she still does to mine, and say, "Corniness is definitely one of the reasons we love you!"

Daddy would snicker and say, "One of the many reasons, right?"

"Right."

Lorraine always came with us everywhere. She was a brindle boxer. She was born on a puppy farm, and when she was tiny, they shut her up in a crate and never let her out. She was stunted and hunched over because of this, and she was a nervous dog. Who could blame her?

The mother of one of Daddy's students had found her and rescued her from the crate, but the family couldn't keep her. The father was allergic. So the student carried the poor abused puppy in his arms, down to the firehouse. I guess the student had Daddy figured for a sucker over dogs. The student was right. We named the dog Lorraine and were very patient with her. Lorraine had had her problems.

"Yes. It's too late. Now, c'mon, girls, we've got things to do," Maggie snapped. She jumped up and walked briskly into the kitchen, leaving me and Amaryllis with the memory jug and the memories.

After the fire—that's when we started house-sitting for people. That's when it became clear to me that people left. Nobody stayed in one place anymore. They used to, I knew they did. I knew lots about what people did a hundred years ago, thanks to Maggie. I knew lots about what people did today, thanks to Daddy and to the people asking us to house-sit for them. They left.

After the fire, after the fire—it seemed that anything bad that happened in our lives came "after the fire."

It was after the fire that we didn't have a dad anymore.

It was after the fire that we didn't have a pet anymore.

It was after the fire that we didn't have a house of our own anymore.

And it was after the fire that we didn't have Amaryllis's voice anymore.

After Amaryllis stopped talking, Maggie took her to

many doctors. Maggie would tell them, "After the fire, after the little ones lost their father, the very morning after the fire—that's when she stopped talking."

I remember that morning. We woke up in a strange room in strange pajamas, Amaryllis and I. Nobody noticed, at first, that she'd stopped talking. We were so busy with grief. But later, we noticed.

The doctors examined Amaryllis. They told Maggie, "Nothing wrong with the child, physically. It's emotional. It's psychological. Try a psychologist."

Maggie took my sister to psychologists. "Perhaps a psychiatrist," they suggested.

Maggie took Amaryllis to a psychiatrist. "Maybe a stay in a nice, soothing environment with professionals that will be able to work with her twenty-four hours a day . . ." suggested the psychiatrist.

Maggie stopped taking Amaryllis to doctors.

"Anyway, I never knew one that didn't need one!" Maggie said about the psychiatrist. "There's nothing we can't work out ourselves. Right, girls?"

"Right, Maggie," I assured her.

Amaryllis smiled and pressed herself into Maggie's hip. She curled around and kissed her tummy, which was about how tall Amaryllis was at the time.

"I don't know any better doctoring than love, than having your own family around you, where they belong," said Maggie.

If they don't leave you first, I thought back then. And I still think so now. Some things don't change.

After the fire, after Daddy died, after we stopped taking Amaryllis to doctors, that was when I started my Special Things Shoe Box. In the beginning, it only had one thing in it. A fireman's medal for bravery. Daddy had earned it long, long ago. Back when I was a kid.

Dad's hero medal was my memory jug. A hero medal, for a quiet hero. A real hero, in my book. Forever and forever.

Chapter 6

The night before the Fourth of July, Maggie and Harry helped the town councilmen, some of whom were women, decorate the town.

When Amaryllis and I walked down to the Lake Shore Road in the clear sunlight of Fourth of July morning, the town was red, white, and blue. Big flags waved in the warm breeze; they lined both sides of the street. Some were tied to the old-fashioned iron streetlights, others were attached to flagpoles that had been specially planted into the crumbly stuff between the sidewalk and the curb.

Shop windows were done up in red, white, and blue

crepe paper with ribbons and bows and golden stars. In the early morning sunlight, storekeepers bent over flowerpots, watering red geraniums, white impatiens, and blue daisies.

"I never heard of blue daisies! Is there such a thing as blue daisies?" I asked Amaryllis.

She gave me a look that said, Well, there they are!

Mr. Platte and the other town councilmembers wore white straw hats with red, white, and blue ribbons around their crowns.

"Wait till the fireworks tonight," he said to me and Amaryllis. "We got *some* grand finale planned!"

"Amaryllis would like to know what a grand finale is," I said. Amaryllis glared at me. "Well, you would, wouldn't you?"

"I'll tell you both," smiled Mr. Platte. "A grand finale is a big ending. A smash of a big, stupendous ending! We had our rockets sent up from North Carolina!" said Mr. Platte, grinning and nodding with pride. "Hey, have you two had Sheila's monkey bread yet?"

He took us into Sheila's Diner and stood us up by the counter. There wasn't an empty table in the place. The radio played "You're a Grand Old Flag," and "America the Beautiful." Ike, Sheila's husband, had the radio turned up loud, and everyone shouted over it. Happy noise filled Sheila's Diner to the ceiling! The walls bulged!

Poppy and Daisy were both helping out behind the counter. They wore cooks' aprons that had bibs and strings that went around back, crisscrossed, then wrapped around and tied in front.

Poppy was in the process of setting out freshly baked sugar and cinnamon doughnuts. She took them from a huge metal tray, which must have been hot because she was wearing a huge, stained red oven mitt on each hand. She placed the doughnuts under glass domes, which steamed up from the heat. Poppy was so tall, her apron barely came to her knees. She was too busy to notice me.

Daisy was pouring orange juice from a huge silver-colored machine into glasses. She was so little, her apron reached her ankles. I hoped she wouldn't have to carry any trays filled with juice to the customers. She'd trip over her apron and the juice would probably end up all over the customers' heads.

Daisy finished pouring, looked up, and saw me. Her eyes zoomed into mine, like magnets. A big smile spread all over her face, she bounced up and down and waved.

I turned away, pretending I didn't notice. As if anyone

would believe that. How could you not notice all that smiling and waving?

Even the jubilant mood of the diner did not make me want to start any ridiculous friendships. I knew what would happen. I'd get involved and then Poppy and Daisy would move away. Just like Michelle moved away.

Mr. Platte ordered Amaryllis and me our very first monkey bread. This was what monkey bread was. It was rolls with lots of thick cinnamon swirled through. Sheila dipped the dough for the rolls into sweet, melted butter. The butter had brown sugar mixed into it. She lumped the rolls into a mound, and sprinkled them with white sugar. Then she baked them. Then she dusted them with confectioner's sugar. Then she set them on a white plate in front of us. She gave us each a bunch of paper napkins.

"She must think we're terribly messy," I whispered to Amaryllis. Then I turned to Mr. Platte and asked, "But why is it called monkey bread?" I saw no monkeys in or around the bread.

"Because this is the way you eat it," answered Mr. Platte. He reached out, grabbed a chunk and stuffed it into his mouth.

"Mmmmmmm," he hummed in sheer delight. "You go after monkey bread like a bunch of monkeys. That's where the name came from," he explained, grabbing another chunk.

"So that's why all the napkins," I said.

"That's why," Mr. Platte agreed, around a mouthful of monkey bread.

Amaryllis and I dug in. The sweet butter rolled down our chins. We dug the thick cinnamon swirls out with the tips of our tongues. We sank our teeth into the bread.

Other people in the world need meat and potatoes, apples, pears and milk, and peas. Monkey bread was enough for me.

Homer's Cove snuggled into a bend in the shoreline of Lake George, like a baby fish in a pebbled nest. There was a park with a beach. It was called Veterans Park.

Veterans Park was next to Ben & Jerry's, across the street from Cobb's Hardware. The park was grass that ran down a big hill, ending up in a sandy beach. Bordering the grass were huge boulders. Some of them had wooden gazebos perched atop. The evening of the Fourth of July, people sat in the gazebos, waiting for the fireworks.

Jutting out from the beach was Homer's Dock. Homer's Dock had a gazebo on it, also. A band was getting itself together under the roof of the gazebo, waiting to play for the people. Every now and then, a *toot* or a *plink* or the *bang* of a drum came from an instrument that a musician was tuning.

It was from Homer's Dock that they launched the boat that would take the fireworks to the raft in the middle of the cove. The fireworks were always set off in this cove, between Homer's Dock and the Northwind Hotel, a big, fancy hotel that jutted out into Lake George on a peninsula.

Maggie and Aunt Sydney and Amaryllis and I walked down to Veterans Park Beach at twilight. Amaryllis had insisted, by laying out our clothes for us, that we all wear red, white, and blue. So the four of us walking that night might have been mistaken for an honor guard for the Grand National Fourth of July Parade.

I had on my royal blue sweatpants. Amaryllis made me wear this lame sweatshirt that Harry had sent our way. Actually, he sent two—one for Amaryllis, one for me.

"Specially for the Fourth," Harry told us, proud of his gift. "These are from my sister. She made them specially for you guys! They're firsts, not seconds. She didn't make any mistakes on these!" Harry beamed.

The sweatshirts were huge. They would have fit Man Mountain Dean. They were white. And a huge flag was sprawled across the front, wrapping around to the back.

"Don't you think it's a little obvious?" I whined to Amaryllis.

She was modeling her flag sweatshirt, which she wore with her red sweatpants. She just smiled, her face alight with the excitement of the evening.

Maggie was dressed all in white. She looked like a star that had fallen down from the sky. Aunt Sydney had on a crisp white blouse and a blue skirt. At the last minute, she had tied a red scarf around her waist. She put a red silk flower in her hair.

"My goodness, Sydney, you look wonderful!" Maggie had told her.

"I wonder if Mr. Platte will be joining us." Aunt Sydney threw the thought out, as if it were a gnat and she was swatting it away. When no one answered her, she said, a bit less nonchalantly, "Ahem. I wonder if Mr. Platte will be joining us."

Maggie looked at me and grinned. I looked at Amaryllis and rolled my eyes. Amaryllis straightened out the red silk flower that was already drooping out of Aunt Sydney's hair.

Twilight turned Lake George into a world of pewter. The lights of the Northwind Hotel reflected on the water, so that there were two hotels, one right side up and the other upside down. Stars glistened in the deep black of the Adirondack sky. We found the huge Big Dipper that floated in the sky at an angle, as if it just finished pouring water into the lake.

Swallows scoured the air above the lake, in search of dinner, and bats poured out of the belfry of the Episcopal church. They skimmed the surface of the lake for snacks.

"Who wants to join us out on the fireworks raft?" drawled Harry. Tonight, he was wearing a red, white, and blue plaid shirt under a green sweatshirt that said EVOC S'REMOH in white letters.

"Oooh, me, me!" I shouted, jumping up and down. I shot my arm straight into the air, to make sure he noticed me.

"Lord, calm down, Mack," said Aunt Sydney.

"Me, me!" I insisted. "Amaryllis, too!"

Harry chuckled. "Well, there's room for everybody, if we squeeze in tight. Climb aboard," he invited us, helping us, one by one, onto his little green runabout.

Aunt Sydney had trouble boarding. She got stuck with one foot in the boat and the other on the dock. The runabout rocked in the wake of a passing boat.

"Lord!" exclaimed Aunt Sydney, falling into the boat,

flat on her rump, her legs sticking straight up in the air. Her skirt flew up, showing off red, white, and blue underpants.

Harry set her upright, grinning a tight grin, trying to hold in a laugh. He couldn't. The laugh burst out from between his closed lips. Maggie joined him in laughing. I did, too. Amaryllis hopped into the boat and smoothed out Aunt Sydney's skirt. She tried to smooth out Aunt Sydney's sense of humor at the same time.

"This is hardly funny. This is . . . this is . . ." spluttered Aunt Sydney. Then she threw up her hands and started laughing. "All right, so it *is* funny. A little," she conceded.

On the ride out to the raft, I asked Harry, "Could we light the fireworks, too? Could we, please, please?"

He shook his head. He'd given up his old blue baseball cap and replaced it with the red cap that Maggie had given him. It was a plain cap, and it looked as if it had been worn for a long time, but it was really new.

When Maggie bought it at Carroll's Department Store she said, "This is a hat that reminds me of Harry. Good, solid, strong and comfortable. It doesn't have that shiny new look." She had fondled the hat lovingly.

"Good grief," I said.

She bought the hat. And now Harry wore it morning, noon, and night.

"No," Harry said, "you can't light the fireworks. But you can watch real close and see how it's done. And maybe in a couple of years, you'll be able to be part of the crew."

"Deal!" I cried. Something tugged at my heart. "But we won't be here in a couple of years. We never stay in one place for that long. It's the way we want it, you know," I said. "We are loose upon the world," I said, remembering my aunt's words.

"Well, we'll see," said Harry.

"Yes, we'll see," Aunt Sydney agreed with Harry.

I looked at Maggie. "We'll see, Mackie," she said.

Only old Harry called me Mackie. And what was all this "we'll see" nonsense?

The boat took off, cutting through the waves toward the fireworks raft. The raft floated in the calm waters in front of the Northwind Hotel. The hotel had many lights lit at night. I'd never visited the Northwind but always looked at it from the Lake Shore Road. Its lights at night made it look like a big ship afloat on the lake.

The Northwind Hotel guests sat in white lawn chairs on the grass that swept a gentle slope, from the porch of the hotel down to the boat docks. Laughter and chatter sprinkled across the lawn, spraying out onto the gently lapping lake. The guests were all atwitter under the fairy lights that twinkled in the trees.

As night darkened Homer's Cove, the boats came in. They came up from Lake George Village and in from the Huddle. Down from Ticonderoga and from the Hague and from Pilot Knob and Log Bay came more boats.

There were big, fancy cabin cruisers and little lake riders. There were sparkly racing boats with mean-looking faces on their bows, which had teenagers aboard in T-shirts and bathing suits. Gray-haired ladies in flower-sprigged dresses and gray-haired gentlemen in seersucker suits were in old-fashioned white wooden boats. The ladies and gentlemen sat in canvas captain's chairs, speaking softly and toasting each other with crystal glasses.

Some houseboats looked like boxes on rafts, and there was a party boat, which was a raft on pontoons. The people on the party boat were definitely having a party! They were very loud and they kept blowing their boat horn and flashing their lights and laughing. Their noise filtered through the darkening air, which calmed the commotion and made it pleasant.

All the boats had lights on them and flags suspended from their bows or hung over their sides. They clustered in the little cove, turned off their motors, and drifted on the gentle waves. They waited patiently for the fireworks to begin and they turned their anchor lights on—little white lights atop their boats. It looked as if a constellation of stars had cascaded down onto the lake. Clusters of shining stars treaded the black waters of Lake George, waiting for the brilliant color of fireworks to take their place in the black Adirondack sky.

All the boats were pointed in toward the land, to get the best view of the show. The green starboard lights on their bows faced us. It was a sea of tiny white lights atop tiny green lights.

As our boat moved toward the raft, we plowed through batteries of bats, taking their supper al fresco. We cut through the soft hills of water and the bats parted for us. We heard the leathery flutter of their wings over our heads. They darted down toward us, pulling up just in the nick of time. They veered off to the left and to the right, in search of delicious morsels of bugs.

We pulled up to the raft. A man already there reached over and caught the line Harry tossed him. Harry hopped out onto the raft and helped Maggie, Aunt Sydney, Amaryllis and, last but not least, me, onto the raft.

From the shore, the music of the band wafted across to the raft. It was time for the fireworks! After each explosion of bangs and color, all the boaters honked their horns in appreciation of the noise and the beauty. Applause flitted like the wings of the bats over the water.

The fireworks exploded in pink fish and purple snakes. Brilliant white novas shattered over the lake. Red stars and green moons and blue comets lit the sky. Their reflections lit the lake. While the fireworks crew sent up rockets from the water, others sent rockets up from the shoreline. Those were smaller fireworks, but no less beautiful. Homer's Cove was brimming with brilliance and bangs.

The fireworks crew got the grand finale rockets ready, for the big ending. The rockets were in cartons marked GRAND FINALE.

The crew struggled with the lighting equipment. They worked and worked, but they could not get the grand finale rockets lit.

The explosions of the other fireworks had taken their echoes and evaporated into the mountain air. The boat horns rested, awaiting their cue for their own grand finale. The bats had given up fighting boats for water-bugs. They had gone back to their belfries, to count the hours until breakfast. The lake was silent in anticipation.

From a boat somewhere on the still lake, a woman sang. Her voice was sweet and strong.

Oh, beautiful for spacious skies,
For amber waves of grain,
For purple mountains' majesty
Above the fruited plain . . .
America, America,
God shed his grace on thee,
And crown thy good
With brotherhood
From sea to shining sea. . . .

The night held its breath. Every boater on the lake, every guest on the Northwind lawn, every citizen of Homer's Cove standing in the sand of Veterans Park Beach, listened.

After the song was finished, boat horns burst alive! People beat their hands together in applause, roaring their appreciation to this lone, unknown singer.

And still we waited for the grand finale fireworks.

"It looks like the works are all wet," said one of the crew.

"How could that have happened? These works have been tucked up tight in the Northwind boathouse," said another.

"Folks, I think the works've been sabotaged," said Harry.

"Who would do such a thing?" asked Maggie.

After the boats had done their share of waiting, and after the news drifted across the cove, that the grand finale fireworks had been sabotaged, the boaters gave up and began to head toward home. They gave one last burst of honks and applause, thanking the fireworks crew for a good show, anyway, and turned on their motors.

The sea of green starboard lights became a sea of red port lights, as the boats turned toward their respective shores.

Harry took us back to shore, kissed Maggie on the nose, and said, "I've got to go back to the raft, to help figure things out."

We thanked Harry and walked through the sand of Veterans Park Beach and up the Lake Shore Road toward home. We passed the people of Homer's Cove who were milling around wondering what had happened to the grand finale fireworks.

I put my hand in my pocket and fingered the piece of rocket shell that the fireworks crew had tossed down onto the raft when they'd finished with it. I had picked it up to put into my Special Things Shoe Box. It would be a memory of the night the stars landed on Lake George.

Chapter 7

To me, Homer's Cove in the rain was as good as Homer's Cove in the sun. That was lucky, because it rained for the four days that followed the Fourth of July. The sea of tourists that had flooded the streets dressed in T-shirts and bathing suits, visiting the little shops, eating fudge from the SugarShack, and playing basketball at Veterans Park, became a stream of tourists in yellow slickers, with their hoods tied close under their chins. In the Grand Union, the checkout lines grew long with whiny children and babies with snot running out of their noses. Older kids hung out under the wide eaves of the Wigwam Shop, loitering and lurking and making nuisances of themselves. It was fun for them to not let older people in and out of the Wigwam easily.

I liked the library in the rain. No one else, apparently, even thought of the library in the rain. I sat in a nice chair with fake leather on it, which felt cool in the summer. I heard the pit-pat of rain dripping on the air-conditioner that stuck out of one of the many windows that filled three of the walls of the library. The air-conditioner was never on.

"Air conditioners are unnecessary in the Adirondacks," stated Miss Marmalyde.

"Well, why does she have an air-conditioner, then?" asked Aunt Sydney, when she heard what the librarian had said.

"One of the Northwind guests donated it," Maggie told her.

"Better off donating books to a library, if you ask me," said Aunt Sydney.

Ms. Marmalyde, the librarian, agreed with her.

For the next four days, I listened to whooshes of wind and the rain beating hard on the tin roof of the library.

"Snug and cozy in here," whispered Miss Marmalyde, who never spoke above a whisper. Not even at home, Harry said.

I felt very at home in the library. In any library, actually. And in all my moving about, I'd seen the inside of plenty of libraries. I discovered that books were the one thing a person could depend on to always be there. And if the particular book that you particularly wanted to read was not there, you knew it would come back in a short time. As opposed to human beings, who once they were gone, were gone for good, libraries protected you from being deserted. As long as you were not bookless, you were not friendless.

You didn't always have to read in the library. You could sit and look out the window at the wet gray sky and the dripping green trees, and you could think.

That is what I did, the rainy days after the Fourth of July. I thought. Who would sabotage the fireworks?

The same answer kept creeping back into my brain.

Shadduck Fey.

That's ridiculous, I would tell that creeping answer, shooing it away with a mental broom.

And still it would creep back.

Shadduck Fey.

Each time the answer came back, it came back a little louder. Finally, it threw itself against the door of my brain that I kept trying to close.

"Ridiculous! He couldn't possibly have done it! He's not smart enough to figure out how to sabotage fireworks. Besides, why would he?" I asked aloud to no one, because no one was in the library except for me and Miss Marmalyde.

"Shhhhh!" warned Miss Marmalyde.

For a minute, I wondered why I had to be quiet when I was the only one there. But the words *Shadduck Fey* continued flinging themselves against my mind, forcing out all other thoughts.

I analyzed it. Why was I so suspicious of him? Really, he'd done nothing bad. Except give Maggie a camel that leaked ink. And splinter apart our front door. And scratch up Maggie's highboy. But he didn't do those things on purpose.

What he did do on purpose was deny that he'd wrecked the door and the highboy, after we'd all seen him with our bare eyes. What he did do on purpose was blame Aunt Sydney for making him help with the highboy. What he did do on purpose was stare at me all through homeroom and math class and art class. What he did do on purpose was lurk around the school at the end of the day, waiting for me, following me home. He tried to hide himself behind the maple trees that lined Horicon

Avenue. He jolted from tree to tree, never realizing that he was highly visible, flinging himself from trunk to trunk. The more a person tried to hide, the more he could be seen. It was better to act normal and have everything out in the open. Then, nobody noticed you. Especially if you were a kid.

Shadduck Fey never figured that out.

I believed there was a chemistry between people that could be very good or very bad. Amaryllis and Maggie and me, we all had excellent chemistry among us. Aunt Sydney and me . . . well, our chemistry was odd. It was like a rosebush, sometimes nice blossoms, sometimes painful thorns. She could be a thorn in my side, and I could be a thorn in her side. A fact of which she reminded me often.

Then there was Shadduck Fey. Shadduck Fey and me. That was bad chemistry.

But to blame him for something like sabotaging the annual Fourth of July fireworks! Why did I have this feeling? "Gut instinct," the television detectives called it.

Who else could it have been?

I splashed home, splattering through the puddles in my soaked sneakers. I thought of all the people I'd come to know in Homer's Cove. There was Mr. Platte, who was like a father to the whole town. He loved Homer's Cove.

It was definitely not Mr. Platte.

I thought of Kee and Laurence, the people that ran Finley's Fancy Restaurant. They were far too busy working all hours of the day and night. Besides, why would they sabotage the grand finale? Laurence was on the fireworks crew. And Kee decked herself out in all red, white, and blue sequins for the entire day and night of the Fourth. Nobody was more excited about the fireworks than Kee and Laurence.

I thought of Mrs. Murphy, the owner of Mary Murphy's Old-fashioned Powder Puff Beauty and Neo-unisex Salon. Anybody who wore her hair as big and high as Mrs. Murphy did, and with as much hair spray and lacquer, would never risk messing it up by going into a musty old boathouse to mess up some fireworks. And she wore pointy spike-heeled shoes. She'd break her neck trying to get into the Northwind Hotel boathouse. She'd have to make it through the marshy boatyard, up the weedy hill, and down the old, cobblestone path to get to where they stored the fireworks.

Mrs. Murphy was not under my suspicion.

I thought of Mrs. Keith and Mrs. Francis. They were far too ancient, and too prim and proper, to do such a thing.

And Sheila and her sister Miss Marmalyde? No way!
Poppy and Daisy Brioche? Too dumb!

Harry? As much as I hated to admit it, Harry did not have a mean blood vessel in his entire vascular system. Harry would let a fly sit on his nose all day long rather than disturb it. Harry may be trying to horn in on our family, upsetting our teamwork, but I had to admit that Harry had honor.

I thought of the kids I'd met at the school. I hadn't been there long enough to get to know any of them well. We didn't move to Homer's Cove until close to the end of the school year. But none of them really seemed mean enough to sabotage a grand finale and disappoint all of Homer's Cove.

There was only one person sneaky enough, sinister enough dishonest enough, to do such a thing.

Shadduck Fey. Shadduck Fey of the lurking, and of the sideways glance at the world, and of the hiding behind trees and fences.

Maggie greeted me at the front door, which Harry had fixed so you couldn't even tell it had been splintered. She had a mop in her hand and a weary smile on her face.

"What's with the mop, Maggie?" I asked. "Is Aunt

Sydney sick?" Mopping was in Aunt Sydney's domain, since she believed she was the only one that knew how.

"No, Aunt Sydney's not sick. Do you think I never houseclean? Well, actually, I wasn't cleaning. The water tank in the cellar seems to have sprung a leak. And, for some reason, the drain in the cellar is plugged up. C'mon, Mack, we've got work cut out for us."

The water in the cellar was up to my knees. Amaryllis and Aunt Sydney stood in the middle of a basement lake, looking like two confused ducks. They each held a mop.

"Good grief," I said.

We plunged in. We took buckets and dunked them and filled them and carried them up the cellar steps and threw the water into the garden, and then we went back for more. And still the water level kept rising.

"Time for a plumber, Maggie," said Aunt Sydney.

"Plumbers cost money. I'm sure we can fix it," said Maggie.

"Do we know plumbing, too?" I asked my mother, unsure of just how far our talents extended.

"Well, if we don't, we'd better learn fast!" said Maggie, in a cheerful, confident voice.

She went over to the water tank and fiddled with it.

She tried to find the floor drain, under all the water.

"I'm sure it was here, somewhere," she said.

Finally, Maggie threw down her mop and her bucket. The mop disappeared into the water; the bucket floated. She shot her fingers through her hair, lifting it back from her face.

"There's only one thing to be done. Come with me, Mack," she said.

I followed her out to the red shed in the backyard. She creaked open the door. It was dark inside. Light seeped in from the open doorway, into the gloom, like a reverse shadow.

"Over here, Mack." She led the way to the side of the barn. She hoisted one end of a canoe up in both her hands.

"Grab that end," she directed.

"Huh?"

"Just grab it, Mackie," she said.

We carried the canoe down into the basement.

"Get in, everybody," said Maggie.

Other people in this life panic. Other people in this life get mad or hysterical or mean. Not my mom!

At first, Aunt Sydney ranted and raved. But there was no putting off Maggie. Her calm spirit soothed everybody around her.

We cruised around the cellar. Maggie sat in one end of the canoe, paddling. I paddled from the other end. Amaryllis sat between Maggie's legs, leaning against her, smiling. Aunt Sydney sat in front of me. After a small fit of fuming, she smiled. A person around my mother could not help but smile.

"Sing a song, Mack," said Maggie.

"Yes, do," said Aunt Sydney.

I sang "Moonlight Bay," which my mother and my aunt had taught me long ago. They used to sing it for my father, in candlelight after dinner. I sang it now, in the flood in our cellar.

We were travelin' along
On Moonlight Bay,
We could hear the voices singing,
They seemed to say . . .
"You have stolen my heart,
Don't go away,"
Da-de-da-da-da-da-da
On Moonlight Bay.

"I forget some of the words," I said.

"Me, too," said Maggie.

"I can't think of them. But sing it again, anyway. Maybe if we all sing it, we'll remember," said Aunt Sydney.

I started, and my aunt joined in, then my mother. We sang together, and Amaryllis swept her fingers back and forth, keeping time and conducting us.

And then our light voices were joined by a deep, rich baritone.

As we sang our old sweet songs
On Moooooonliiiiiight Baaaaayyyy.

"You are really some kind of woman, Maggie-girl." Harry stood at the top of the cellar steps, grinning down at us. "Maggie-girl," he said again, softly.

Good grief! I thought. As if a flood weren't enough!

By the time Harry, with Maggie's help, had fixed the water tank problem and unclogged the drain, he'd stuck himself right onto our family.

Like a wart.

Chapter 8

Shadduck Fey made himself scarce for the rest of the summer. Mr. Platte, whom I saw a lot around Homer's Cove, told me Shadduck was visiting his aunt in Glens Falls.

Harry told me Shadduck was visiting his aunt down in Albany.

Sheila told me Shadduck was visiting his aunt up at Lake Placid.

Mrs. Keith said Shadduck was visiting his aunt out in Rochester.

"Shadduck Fey certainly has his share of aunts," I

said, sitting at the counter at Shirley's Diner. Amaryllis sat beside me, and together we plunged into an order of monkey bread.

"Shadduck has a large family," Sheila agreed.

"Shadduck has a large guilty conscience," I whispered to Amaryllis, licking my fingers. She shrugged her shoulders, licking her own fingers.

I turned to face my sister squarely. Her delicate profile was dark against the sunlight that poured in through the diner windows. Her hair was pulled back in pink barrettes, to keep it out of the monkey bread. She had learned to eat it very well; there were fewer butter traces on her chin than on mine.

"Well, don't you agree?" I asked her.

She shrugged her shoulders again. This was not like Amaryllis, to not agree with me. I continued to face her, willing her to turn and agree with me. She continued to eat, as if I was no longer there.

Amaryllis had developed a talent lately to ignore me. Amaryllis, upon whom I could always depend to hang onto my every word and to follow my every direction . . . Amaryllis seemed to be changing.

This year had been filled with changes—a change of home (Homer's Cove), a change of family (Aunt Sydney), a change of team composition (Harry). And now it seemed as if Amaryllis was changing, too!

Summer passed through Homer's Cove in warm breezes that tickled the white sails of sailboats, and in sunlit days and star-strewn nights. Homer's Cove burst at its seams with tourists.

Our little house on Maple Street burst at its seams with more and more antiques. Maggie's business was doing well.

"Bring in more dust, why don't you?" complained Aunt Sydney, swiping with her dust rags at each new old dust-covered antique Maggie brought home.

I kept busy helping Maggie, going on her antique "treasure hunts" with her, lugging stuff in and out with her. We had become a team again. Harry was busy building docks.

"I hardly get to see Harry anymore. He's so busy. But I am glad his business is doing so well," said Maggie.

"Thank heaven for small favors," I said.

"It's nice that you're so interested in his success, Mackie," Maggie said.

"I'm interested only because it's keeping him out of my hair," I retorted.

"Swell attitude."

I shrugged.

Since we spent so many days on the road, scouting out new places to get antiques, visiting houses and shops, I didn't see many of the kids from school. Occasionally, I saw a clump of girls that hung out and did each other's hair and laughed and generally acted silly, all in Stewart's parking lot. They reminded me of Iris and Julia, the popular girls I had known down in Lake George Village. Usually there was a clump of boys cavorting in the parking lot, too, showing off for the girls. Shades of Shadduck Fey.

One afternoon in August, I was on the front porch, swinging on a ramshackle porch swing Maggie had found in a seedy little junk shop over the mountain, in Ticonderoga. It had a slat back with most of the slats missing. Its seat was the same. On every swing back and forth, it squeaked like a suffering rodent,

Maggie had been so proud when she carted it home.

"Look at this! Isn't it great?! Where should we put it?" she asked with her usual enthusiasm.

"The village dump?" Aunt Sydney offered with her usual cynicism.

For once, I agreed with Aunt Sydney—but I kept it to myself.

"Don't worry. Harry will have it shipshape in no time, soon's his busy season is over," Maggie said.

"By then, it'll be too cold to use it," I reasoned.

"Absolutely," agreed Aunt Sydney.

"Killjoys," scoffed Maggie at us. "His busy season will be over soon enough!"

Good grief, I thought. Please, God, let his busy season never be over.

That afternoon in August, I was cooling my heels, or trying to, by swinging mightily back and forth, back and forth on the porch swing. I was practicing scales on my flute and making up little tunes. I was trying to match the songs of the birds that filled our backyard in the early mornings.

"Hi, there!" I heard a voice say. I looked across the porch. Poppy and Daisy stood on the steps, grinning and nodding their blossomy heads.

"Hey," I said, making sure they saw my extreme and total disinterest.

"Wanna play? We've got our Kelly dolls. See?" said Poppy, offering out her large hand on which sat two pint-sized dolls that looked like stunted Barbie dolls.

Daisy chimed in, "We'd be happy to share. That is, if you don't have any Kelly dolls of your own."

"What's a Kelly doll?" I asked, scowling.

Ignoring my scowl, Daisy bounced up onto the porch, chirping like a bluebird. Poppy clumped up behind her, her head at full tilt and a huge smile spread across her face.

"These are Kelly dolls," Daisy explained. "Kelly one and Kelly two and Kelly three—" she said, pointing to the dolls Poppy held and holding out her own.

I interrupted, "Just how old are you?" I asked, sounding more like Aunt Sydney in one of her moods than I wanted to. But after all . . . Kelly dolls!

Poppy said, "I'm eleven. Daisy's twelve."

"And you're still playing with dolls?" I spat.

Poppy looked at Daisy and Daisy looked at Poppy. They both looked at me.

Daisy shrugged and said, "Sometimes. It's still kind of fun, you know? Besides, they're really not just dolls. They're . . . they're . . . um . . . collectibles."

"Yeah, right," I grimaced.

The girls' smiles evaporated into the August air. I had done that.

Poppy said, "Mack Humbel, why are you so unfriendly? We're just trying to make friends, and you are so unfriendly!"

"I don't need friends."

"Everybody needs friends," said Poppy. Daisy nodded.

"Not me, baby," I said confidently, acting like a gangster, folding my hands in back of my head, my elbows sticking up into the air. All I needed was a fat cigar in my mouth.

"Well," said Daisy.

"Well," said Poppy

"Well?" said me.

"Well, we tried," said Poppy, rolling her eyes and shrugging her shoulders. "We tried to be friends, and you always act so stuck-up! I don't know what your problem is!"

"Yeah. What is your problem, anyway?" said Daisy.

"I don't have a problem!" I shouted. "I just want to be left alone!"

"Fine!" said Daisy and Poppy together. And together, they turned and flounced off the porch. Poppy flounced considerably less than Daisy.

I sat in the hot August afternoon, all by myself, and wondered if I were a fool.

They said I was stuck-up! I'm not stuck-up. I have never, ever been stuck-up! Iris and Julia were stuck-up. Certainly, not me. I just minded my own business.

Maggie likes me the way I am. Amaryllis likes me. Michelle liked me. Daddy loved me. Exactly as me.

Oh, well. Let them hate me, if they did. Let them! What did I need them for? Michelle left. Daddy left. I needed no more encumbrances, to get me all involved and then to leave me!

I picked up my flute, put it to my lips, then let it fall down onto my lap. I didn't play anymore that afternoon.

By Labor Day, the sabotaging of the grand finale had become a part of Homer's Cove history. It was accepted that no one would ever know who had done it, or why. It was accepted as one of Homer's Cove's mysteries.

I kept my suspicions to myself.

Even more tourists poured onto the beach at Veteran's Park, to celebrate Labor Day, the last weekend of the summer. A party of campers brought in a whole pig on a spit. They turned it slowly over a campfire. It turned for the whole day.

"It's very gross-looking," I said.

"But delicious!" said Harry.

"And it smells so good!" said Maggie.

"It's a tradition," said Mrs. Murphy, who had closed up her beauty parlor and left her spike heels at home for once.

She wore a beach robe that was layers of lavender chiffon, and thin-strapped silver sandals. Her hair was still in piles of blond curls atop her head. She had on black sunglasses shaped like cats' eyes. The frames were encrusted with rhinestones. Mrs. Murphy glistened and sparkled.

"They killed the pig themselves," said Mrs. Keith and Mrs. Francis.

"They take all day to roast a pig every year but never take time to visit the library," Ms. Marmalyde whispered. She was wearing a tent dress of turquoise, with purple and pink dragons curling around on it. Her sunhat was broadbrimmed, and the crown was covered in the same material as her dress.

I sat in the sand between Ms. Marmalyde and Aunt Sydney. We three relaxed in striped canvas sand chairs. Aunt Sydney wore a gray bathing suit with white trim. The suit had a high neck and a big skirt on it. Aunt Sydney was very covered up. We sat sipping iced tea quickly, before the ice melted. We buried our toes in the sand and turned our faces up to the sun. I closed my eyes and listened to the purr of gossip between Ms. Marmalyde and Aunt Sydney.

Amaryllis was wading in the lake. Maggie and Harry stood at the shore, watching her.

Mrs. Keith and Mrs. Francis closed Carroll's Department Store for the day. They asked Cobb from Cobb's Hardware to carry their porch rockers to Veterans Park Beach. He put the rockers by our sand chairs. The rockers sank into the sand. The ladies sat primly and properly in polka-dot dresses and straw hats with flowers and in straight-backed wooden chairs that were no longer rockers. They chattered with each other, two magpies, and gossiped with the other grown-ups. Mrs. Francis laughed a lot; Mrs. Keith grumbled a lot.

Aunt Sydney and Maggie had packed a huge basket of food for the Labor Day picnic, enough for everybody in Homer's Cove! There was chicken salad and potato salad and macaroni salad with white chunks of tuna fish in it. There was a watermelon scooped out, so the shell of the watermelon was shaped like a basket with a handle. Inside were orange cantaloupe balls and green honeydew melon balls and red watermelon balls. I put in blueberries, remembering how good Homer's Cove had looked for the Fourth, in its red, white, and blue. Amaryllis tossed in miniature marshmallows, for the white.

"Good thinking, Amaryllis," I complimented her.

There was fried chicken with a thick and crispy crust. It crumbled in pumpkin-colored crumbs when you bit in.

Amaryllis, Maggie, and Harry raced each other to the picnic basket. I joined them, threw the basket open, and we dug in. There was much passing around of plates and of compliments.

"Oh, look at that fruit basket. Isn't that the most wonderful thing, Mrs. Keith?" asked Mrs. Francis, clapping her hands. Although they were sisters, Mrs. Keith and Mrs. Francis always addressed each other formally.

"Humpf!" said Mrs. Keith. "That took a lot of work!"

"Indeed!" agreed her sister.

"What luscious looking salads," whispered Ms. Marmalyde.

"Here, let me help you," offered Aunt Sydney, passing the librarian a red paper plate.

"Oh, I really shouldn't. I'm dieting," said Ms. Marmalyde.

"No diets on a grand picnic like this," said a mild, masculine voice.

"Hey, Mr. Platte!" I called, running over to him. I took him by the hand and dragged him over. He made believe he was protesting, but he came pretty easily.

Aunt Sydney jumped up, smoothing her hair with one hand and the skirt of her old-fashioned bathing suit with the other.

"Do join us, please, Mr. Platte," she gushed.

"You're getting too much sun, Aunt Sydney. You're turning all red," I pointed out to her.

She looked daggers at me, then turned back to Mr. Platte and led him over to the open basket. She heaped a ton of food on his plate. I overheard him say to her, "Please call me Norman."

Amaryllis and I feasted on fried chicken. Our fingers glistened with grease.

"That's what's nice about picnics at the beach. You can jump in the lake to wash off. Right, Amaryllis?" I asked.

"Oh, go jump in a lake!" Harry said, chuckling.

Amaryllis polished off a whole half of a chicken, threw the bones into the garbage bag, and plunged back into the water she'd just left. She was laughing. Almost out loud. Maggie watched her like a hawk, as if she expected sound to come out of her at any given moment.

Because Maggie watched her, Harry watched her, too.

Harry brought a chocolate upside-down cake.

"My specialty," he said, shoving a huge piece at Maggie. As if she would ever eat it all. Maggie was a very picky eater.

She ate it all.

121

Aunt Sydney warned, "You'll become quite round if you eat like that, Maggie."

"Round is nice, too." Harry absolutely gleamed when he looked at Maggie. Maggie gleamed right back.

Amaryllis rejoined us and had a piece of Harry's specialty, then had seconds.

"Good grief!" I said to myself. I sucked on a lemon.

Then Amaryllis and I ran down to the shore and jumped and splashed into the cool water of the lake. We dunked each other and she climbed up on my shoulders and I plunged her over backward.

Sheila must have closed up the diner for the afternoon, because she and her husband, Ike, were in their bathing suits in the water, splashing and laughing with Poppy and Daisy. They were having a grand old time—a family of four. They looked so happy.

Poppy and Daisy saw me and stared. I stared back. They turned their backs to me. My heart shriveled a little.

There were kids that I recognized from school, swimming in clusters around us. I'd show Poppy and Daisy! I'd join the other kids and make those two girls sorry they ever called me stuck-up! I moved toward some of the kids. I stopped before I got too close.

Why bother? I asked myself. Who cares? It's too late, anyway. Poppy and Daisy already hate me. And, besides, we won't be staying in Homer's Cove long enough to get to really know anybody. And I'm too busy helping Maggie. And I'm too busy getting Amaryllis to talk. I'm too busy trying to keep intruders out! I reasoned.

I looked at Harry, and at Aunt Sydney, and now at Mr. Platte. We were going from a pint-sized family to an extra-large king-sized one. What would I do with more people in my life? Enough is enough!

The sun baked us, the water cooled us, the breeze swept cold over our soaked hair. Little laps of waves sparkled in the sunlight.

We ran back to our spot on the beach and burrowed into the sand. I lay on my stomach and closed my eyes tight. I saw the inside of my eyelids. They were black-red and felt hot.

The warmth of the sun was a thing I could almost touch. It encased me in a shell. I was a clam in my own little house of heat. The sounds of the beach drifted away, outside the walls of my shell. I heard soft music from radios, happy laughter from children, twiny vines of gossip from older people. I smelled the coconut of suntan oil. I was inside the sun, and everything was secure and safe and nothing would move or leave. It was a moment I wanted to last forever.

"Mack Humbel," a voice whined, weaseling itself into my sun house.

"Mack Humbel," the voice persisted, bringing me back from my safe haven.

"Mack Humbel," insisted Shadduck Fey.

He stepped close to me. His shadow blocked out the sun. I got a severe chill.

"Wanna go for a walk?" he asked.

"No!" I answered.

"Why not?" he asked.

"Go away!" I demanded.

"Aw, c'mon," he wheedled.

"Persistent, aren't you?" I remarked, rolling over, sitting up, and brushing sand off my knees.

"Now, Mackie, go ahead. After all, Shadduck's been away all summer," said Aunt Sydney, obviously forgetting that Shadduck Fey had called her a prune during the highboy incident.

"Aunt Sydney, did you call me Mackie? Please, please, my name is Mack!" Harry was affecting everybody.

My aunt clicked her tongue and clucked, "Just go. Be polite."

I looked around me. Amaryllis snored into the sand, blowing little granules this way and that. Maggie and Harry sat on a towel, on another planet.

"Lord!" I said, sounding more like Aunt Sydney than I cared to. I got up with a grunt, to show my displeasure at having been disturbed, and turned to Shadduck. "If I go for a walk with you, you have to walk ten paces away from me, to my left. And at least five paces behind me."

"Okay," he agreed.

"C'mon, then," I said.

Alongside of Veterans Park, there was a labyrinth of boulders spread out under giant oak and evergreen trees. Picnic tables were scattered here and there, but the picnickers had left the shade of the trees and were sweating down on the beach. Shadduck and I had the labyrinth to ourselves.

We fished our way through rock passages, which were dark and cool. We climbed rickety wooden stairs that somebody had put in between the rocks, long ago. We came out on the top of the tallest boulder. There was a gazebo perched on the rock, overlooking the lake. It had benches along its open-air sides. Shadduck sat down on a bench, facing the water. He was huffing and puffing and all sweaty.

"Out of shape, Shadduck?" I inquired, a mean grin curling my lips. "Please note that I'm not even breathing hard."

"You're a good climber, Mackie," he panted.

I jumped at him and grabbed the front of his shirt. I shook him. "Don't you ever EVER call me Mackie! My name is M-A-C-K!!"

"Okay, okay! Sorry! Jeeesh!" Shadduck whined.

I walked over to the rail that went along the front of the gazebo. I put my hands on the rail and gripped it. I looked out over the lake. From here, you could see Dome Island. There were always a lot of little boats around Dome Island, because that's where the fishermen caught the most land-locked salmon and the most smallmouth bass. Cobb from Cobb's Hardware told me this. Cobb was very impressed with Dome Island.

"There's a wreck on the bottom, out there," he told me, nodding in the direction of the island.

"A wreck of what?" I asked.

"A boat," he answered.

"What boat?" I asked. Getting information from Cobb was like pulling teeth with a set of his pliers. Except if the information was about fishing. Then he talked a lot.

"The old steamboat *Mohican*. It used to be a dinner

cruise boat. People would get all gussied up and boat up and down the lake, eating fancy food and dancing and singing. One night, the *Mohican* got too close to the shore of Dome Island, rammed itself on a tree fallen under the surface of the water, and sank. Nobody was drowned, but a lot of the ladies lost their jewels. Still down there, in the wreckage. When the sunlight hits the water right, you can see the ribs of the boat. Some say you can see the sparkle of the jewels."

"The ribs?"

"The skeleton."

"The skeleton?"

"Yup." And Cobb was finished talking.

"But why doesn't anybody dive for the jewels?" I asked.

Cobb shrugged. Definitely finished talking.

I stood in the gazebo and looked out to Dome Island. There were many boats anchored along its edge. They looked like seagulls, brilliant in their white, perched on the waves, waiting for fish to come along to gobble down for dinner.

To the left of Dome Island, the Northwind gleamed in the sun. It jutted out into the clear blue waters like a swan.

Behind Dome Island was Log Bay. Harry promised to take us over there all summer, but we never made it. He was too busy with the dock building and whatever. Log Bay was supposed to be excellent swimming. You could reach it only by boat. You anchored and jumped out. The water was shallow, and the sands on the bottom of the bay were like silk under your feet. Or so they said.

Way off to the right of Dome Island, trees stuck out of the water. There were leafy trees and also evergreens. They were actually on an island so tiny, you could only see the things on it and not the island itself. This was Tea Island. It got its name because the ladies who lived in a great mansion down there used to boat out to Tea Island every afternoon for tea and scones and jam and cream.

Mrs. Keith and Mrs. Francis told me this, when Maggie was buying Harry's hat. Mrs. Keith also told me that one of the ladies of the mansion had killed her children, but that's all they would tell me about her.

"Some way to leave off a story. Why bring it up at all?" I grumbled to Maggie on the way to Harry's to deliver the hat. I kicked at twigs along the road, complaining with my feet as well as with my mouth.

"Mrs. Keith and Mrs. Francis both like their intrigue. They both like their mysteries," Maggie said.

From the gazebo, I felt I was surveying my kingdom. I felt power. I felt that now was a good time to get to the bottom of the Fourth of July grand finale fiasco.

"So, Shadduck. You did it, didn't you? You sabotaged the Fourth of July fireworks." I stood with my back to Shadduck, looking out to Dome Island.

I felt Shadduck tense. I sensed that he stepped backward, away from me.

"No . . . no . . . uh . . . uh . . ." he stuttered.

"I know you did it! Confess!"

"But I didn't mean it. It was an accident. Don't tell anybody, pleeeeeaaaaassssssee!" he whined.

"HAH! I knew it! You are the perpetrator! You are the culprit! You, sir, are the guilty party!" I shouted, pointing my finger at him in one of my finer melodramatic moments.

"But I didn't mean it. I only wanted to figure out how to work the rockets," he whined some more.

"Oh, really. And why would you want to do that?" I asked, in my best, most important lawyer's voice.

"I wanted to impress you! I heard Mr. Goodwell say he was bringing you out to the fireworks raft for the display. I was going, too. My cousin's Jake who lights the rockets. I figured if I could push Jake aside at the last minute and light the grand finale rockets myself, I'd impress you. If I'd asked Jake to let me, he'd never go for it. I'm under the age, y'know."

"Huh! You wanted to impress me? Are you out of your mind?" I shouted. I couldn't believe this!

He nodded fiercely and pitifully. "I thought you might go to the movies with me," he sniveled, almost in tears. He continued, "Then, when I got in the boathouse, I pulled the cartons of fireworks out of the tarps and it was too much and my hands were too sweaty and everything was slippery and the boxes fell through the fish hatch hole in the boathouse floor!" Shadduck was whimpering by this time. "I caught the tarp corners, right at the last minute, but everything inside got dunked." He was sobbing now. "I hadda run all the way home and sneak out my mother's blow dryer. I hadda blow dry the fireworks!"

"Good grief! You mean the Fourth of July grand finale got screwed up because of ME???!!!?"

This idea appealed to him. He stopped sobbing and sniffled greatly. Several times over.

"Yeah. That's right. It was actually kind of your fault, Mack Humbel. So you better never tell. You're actually an accomplice to the crime," spat smarmy Shadduck Fey.

I felt him come up close behind me.

"Um, uh, Mack Humbel, um . . ."

"Out with it, Fey!" I shouted.

"Um, uh . . ."

"What?!" my word jabbed at him like a jackknife. It was enough to spur him to do what he wanted to do. It moved him to do something that was as far away from my mind as the planet Pluto.

He grabbed me by the shoulder and spun me around. His fingers jabbed in under my shoulder bone.

"Hey, that hurts!" I cried.

Then he pulled at me. My foot struck a loose board in the gazebo floor and I stumbled toward him.

And then he kissed me. His kiss hit me smack in the temple, right next to my eye. If it had been half an inch to the left, his pointy nose would have poked my eye out.

"Yuck!" I screamed, and smacked him in the head, and again in the gut.

"OOOOffff!" he huffed.

"Eeeewww!" I screamed again, tearing at my temple with my knuckles, trying to get the disgusting feel of the kiss out of my skin.

"Ow!" he groaned. "You hurt my stomach."

"You are gross and disgusting, Shadduck Fey!" I told

131

him. I pushed him down onto the gazebo floor, and I turned and ran. I flew down through the labyrinth, through the picnic tables, past the people on the beach. I leaped over picnic baskets and crumpled towels. I side-swiped baby carriages and garbage cans and ran through the park and out onto the sidewalk and across the busy street. Cars honked at me and drivers shouted and I never once stopped; I never once looked back.

I didn't slow down until I got myself through my front door. I slammed it shut and locked it and leaned back against it, sweating and panting, my heart pounding as if it were trying to fly out of my chest.

Kissed by Shadduck Fey! My life was over!

Chapter 9

E WG was a fine word. It was an excellent word. It was a word you could sink your teeth into. You got to screw up your face and go, "Ewg. Eeeew-wwwgggg. EeeeewwwwwwwwwwwwwwwwwwG!"

It was a word that I made up, after the Kiss. It stood for what I felt. It was synonymous with "yuck."

EWG also stood for Extremely Weird Group.

The Extremely Weird Group was a group of students at school. I hadn't taken much notice of them when I entered Homer's Cove School last spring. But I noticed them plenty the fall that I entered eighth grade.

EWG had no leader. But EWG did have a center. At

the center was the weirdest of them all, Shadduck Fey. EWG had no schedule to follow; no place they hung out at together; they had no life of their own. They just had a way of annoying people. They were like an octopus. Its head alone was effectless and dull, with nothing important going on inside of it. But give it tentacles of annoyance probing into everything . . . that's another story.

EWG people did things like study for a test for a zillion hours and still only get a seventy on it. And then be happy that they just passed! They never did anything significant, like get a 110 percent, or like bomb out and get a minus zero. EWGs wallowed in mediocrity.

There had been a border-EWG group back in the Lake George school. Michelle and I used to watch them and they had made us giggle. They had a way of falling off science lab stools and used to accidentally walk into their own locker doors, by pulling them open and stepping too quickly and too close at the same time. But Michelle and I had never made a name for them. We had been too young—only third graders!

The EWGs I observed at Homer's Cove School snorted during laughter and sprayed during speech. They wore ace bandages around wrists or ankles that didn't need them, just to look like heroes. EWG people were not brave. And they were not friendly, either. Not that I cared. I had no room in my gypsy life for friends.

Pamela Bowe was an EWG. She was chubby and had dull brown hair that hung down her back in a clumpy braid. She had large ears and no apparent personality.

She lived four houses down from us, in a white house on the corner. From her porch, she could see the school.

Maggie said, "Such a nice, quiet girl," about Pamela Bowe.

Aunt Sydney said, "Yes. Very nice. Very quiet." Then she looked at me. With meaning.

Pamela Bowe floated like a ghost around the outskirts of the EWGs. She was not at the center of the group, like Shadduck Fey.

"She doesn't have enough personality to be at the center of anything," I commented about her to Amaryllis.

But Amaryllis took a liking to Pamela Bowe. Amaryllis ran to catch up with her in the mornings, on the way to school. Amaryllis left me behind.

"I don't run to catch up with anybody," I called after her. "I don't have to!" I yelled.

Pamela Bowe and Amaryllis walked to school together in silence. I trailed behind and filled in the silent air with chatter. I sounded like a squirrel.

"You sound like a nut," said Shadduck Fey, one late September morning. He was lurking under a maple tree. The tree sent down helicopters of seeds, twirling to the sidewalk. Shadduck stuck one on his nose.

He said, "Did you notice you're talking to yourself? Nobody's listening!"

"Shut up!" I said.

One morning while we were parading to school in the usual fashion, Amaryllis and Pamela up front, me plodding behind, Pamela turned back and said to me, "Your sister's sure quiet."

"So you finally noticed," I spat at her. "Well, why walk to school with her, then?" I yelled.

"I like quiet people," Pamela stated. Pamela was a very confident person. She gave me a look and then turned around and smiled at my sister.

"Well, my mother says Amaryllis is choosy about whom she talks to," I told Pamela. "So she might never talk to you!"

Both Pamela and Amaryllis turned around and looked at me in surprise. Maybe I was going over the edge. Maybe I was being a bit too touchy. So I tried to grin, as if it had all been a joke. I chuckled. The whole thing went over like a lead balloon. Good grief!

Pamela slowed down and waited for me to catch up. Amaryllis slowed down, too.

Pamela said to me, "Shadduck said you call your mother by her first name."

"Uh-huh," I said, boring quickly with the conversation.

"Do you call your mother by her first name?" Pamela asked Amaryllis.

Amaryllis looked at her. She rolled her eyes. My sentiment, exactly, I agreed with Amaryllis in my mind.

Pamela snorted. Amaryllis smiled. I slowed way down, putting the distance back between them and me.

In late October, we crunched our way to school through piles of bronze and golden leaves. Amaryllis ran ahead and plunged into the leaves, the way she had plunged into Lake George only weeks before.

"The change of seasons is definite and distinct in the Adirondacks and falls swiftly," Mr. Platte told me.

I liked being in the Combined Seventh & Eighth. I got to have Mr. Platte again for homeroom, and I had all the same teachers as last year for the rest of the subjects. I heard some of the kids moaning because they had some hated teachers for the second full year in a row. But since

I'd entered Homer's Cove School only late last spring, I didn't have time to feel one way or another about the teachers. I just knew I didn't have to learn any new names. It was a break, and I needed all the breaks I could get.

I looked out a window in homeroom, down at the lake.

"When will the lake freeze?" I asked Mr. Platte.

"Not for quite a while, yet. Anxious to go skating?" he asked.

"I want to sleigh ride down Horicon hill! You remember, Mr. Platte? We talked about it. Sledding down Horicon hill! Zoom! Right out onto Lake George!" I flailed my arms about, describing the way my sled would fly.

Mr. Platte frowned. "Now, hold on. We agreed that was not a good idea. Didn't we, Mack Humbel." The last thing he said was not a question, but a statement.

"Yes, Mr. Platte," I said.

"I mean it, Mack."

"Yes, Mr. Platte," I said again.

After school, I had band practice. After that, I stood beneath the flag, my arms filled with books and papers and my flute in its case. I stared down the great hill, out onto the lake. It surely would have been a trip, on a good sled with freshly waxed runners! What a trip it would have been!

Amaryllis didn't wait for me on the days I had band after school, so I headed home by myself. Amaryllis was there sitting hunched on the bottom step of the front porch, along with the wonderful Pamela Bowe. Their feet and ankles were submerged in dried, golden leaves. They were pumping their legs up and down, like pistons in an engine. They were stomping leaves. Pamela Bowe was teaching Amaryllis to snort when she laughed.

"Snorting takes noise. Amaryllis doesn't have noise!" I said.

"That's how much you know," said Pamela Bowe in a snotty voice.

"You don't have to be so touchy," I said.

"You don't have to be so bossy," she said.

I sucked my teeth, then gulped down air and gave her a major belch."That's what I think of what you know, Pamela Bowe!" I said.

Amaryllis shook her head and rolled her eyes.

"C'mon, 'Ryllis, let's make more leaf wine," Pamela said.

"Number one, her name is *Ama*ryllis," I started,

counting on my fingers like Maggie did. "And number two, what is leaf wine?"

"Leaf wine! Leaf wine!" Pamela Bowe cried, extending her arms, jerking them up and down, holding out her hands to me, palms up, as if in explanation. She started pumping her legs again. She definitely manifested strong EWG mannerisms.

"What a jerk," I mumbled to myself.

Her October-colored boots smushed the leaves at her feet into pulp.

"It's like stomping grapes into wine, Mack. The way they do in Italy. But we're stomping leaves instead of grapes. The way we do in Homer's Cove! C'mon, it's fun!" she cried, inviting me to join them.

Amaryllis pumped her legs, stomping leaves into leaf wine. Her shoulders shook in silent laughter. She clapped her hands. She looked like she had forgotten I was there.

Harry's pickup truck pulled up, and Harry lumbered out, first the red hat, then a red sweatshirt, then the rest of him.

He asked us, "You like the sweatshirt your mom gave me?"

Proudly, he pulled out its hem, so our eyes could

feast on it. "It doesn't say anything! Isn't that great?!"

"Good grief," I told him.

"Hey! You girls making leaf wine?" Harry asked, delighted. He chuckled and scratched my head. He scratched Amaryllis's head and then Pamela's head on his way up the stairs.

"What are we, dogs?" I mumbled.

Harry Goodwell did not ring the doorbell anymore. He simply knocked real loud and barged his way into my house, without waiting for an invitation. Just like he barged his way into my life.

Pamela Bowe got up, brushed leaf fragments off her ankles, and followed Harry into my house.

"Hey!" I cried. "Doesn't anybody believe in invitations anymore?!"

Amaryllis followed Pamela into the house. She didn't look at me, at all.

Other people in the world had control of their lives. I used to be one of those people. I used to have Maggie. I used to have Amaryllis. I used to have a team. Long ago, I even used to have a father.

Now I had nothing. Except for intruders. And I was getting the idea that none of them really liked me. They simply came in and exploded my life into all different directions, leaving me standing alone on a front porch in a house that wasn't even mine.

There were times in life when minutes kicked up their heels and flew by, like rockets. For instance, when you needed extra time to double-check on a math test, because if you flunked the test, you'd get a failure on your permanent record, which would follow you around for life. Or so they said. At those times, minutes laughed in your face and raced away, leaving you with no time at all. There were other times when minutes became snails and crawled by. "Look at me!" they called to you. "I'm not letting time go by at all. We're at a standstill here!" For instance, in the hour before lunch in social studies class, when you're so hungry even cafeteria food sounds good, and all you want to do is eat cheeseburgers or pizza, and instead you're being fed names and dates and names and dates and it's so boring!

Now minutes were snails as I sat in our living room and watched Harry and Maggie grin at each other.

Harry had brought along pumpkins for us to carve.

"Let me go back out to the truck and bring 'em in," he shouted jovially.

"Oh, these are beautiful pumpkins, Harry," Maggie exclaimed when she saw them.

"Grew 'em myself," Harry boasted, his face bursting with smiles and pride.

"Oh, Harry!" Maggie beamed.

In my mind, I groaned and moaned in nausea.

Harry lived in a deep-green house about a mile from our house. His front porch was tan and was always crammed with tools and with junk that he found when he made the treasure-hunt circuit with Maggie. The junk he dragged home, though, was mostly old fishing poles and nets and reels and stuff. Very boring; very ugly.

Harry had a huge garden. From the size of it, you'd think he was feeding all of Lake George, including the fish and the seagulls. Harry lived alone, but he loved a good, big garden. In my book, it wasn't even a real garden. It just had vegetables in it. The only flowers were the marigolds he planted around the edges.

"Their bitter smell keeps pests away," he explained.

"Then maybe I'd better plant marigolds all around Maggie," I said.

I got into big trouble with Maggie for that one. But Harry just laughed.

Amaryllis and Pamela Bowe sat together at the end of the couch, looking over Harry's pumpkins. It was very quiet down there, on their end.

Then Pamela said, "I just love to carve out jack-o'-lanterns!"

Aunt Sydney, who was spreading old newspaper under the pumpkins, turned to Pamela and said, "Then you must stay and help us carve them, dear."

"Okay," Pamela said.

Amaryllis smiled.

Piece by piece, my life was falling apart.

Chapter 10

Halloween morning-thick frost had covered the lawns of Homer's Cove the night before. In the crisp air, the village looked as if it had been powdered with sugar. Frost glittered over orange pumpkins and orange lawn-and-leaf bags, stuffed to full and scattered over yards in decoration for the feast of ghosts and goblins. It glittered over clumps of brass-colored leaves that had escaped the rakes of the people who tended their lawns. Under our heavy shoes, the frost broke like thousands of tiny crystal glasses as we walked up Horicon hill to school on Halloween morning.

"Going to be a cold winter, Mackie!" shouted Harry, as he sailed by me in his pickup.

"What are you going to be for Halloween?" asked Shadduck Fey, panting up the hill behind me.

"Let me guess what you're going to be. An EWG?"

"What's that?" he asked.

"Guess."

"Uh . . . a computer thing?"

"Yeah, sure," I said, skimming through the school door and letting it slam in his face. Then I looked around, hoping no one had seen me do that.

Oh, well, he's just an EWG, I rationalized.

Still, I went to school that day with a sour taste in my mouth, brought about by my own thoughtless actions.

I had walked to school alone on Halloween morning, and I walked home alone after school on Halloween afternoon. I found Maggie standing at an old desk she'd just gotten. She had placed it in front of the TV, so you could hear a man's voice tell how to make your toilet bowl sparkle like diamonds, but you couldn't see him or the toilet.

Maggie leaned against the desk, studying a letter she held in her hand. She gripped the envelope in her other hand.

"What's the matter, Maggie?" I asked.

"The school. They want to see me. About Amaryllis. She doesn't talk," said Maggie. She sounded surprised, as if the fact that Amaryllis didn't talk came as a shock. As if she expected the letter to speak up and explain itself.

I said, "But she does her work. She gets good grades. What's their problem?" I asked.

"They think there's something wrong with her," Maggie said.

"Just go tell them there isn't," I told her.

"Easier said than done."

"I'll go with you," I offered.

"Thanks, pal. But maybe Harry should go with me," she murmured.

"Why do we need him?" I asked.

"Well, because. You know. Because, you know," she explained. "Go get Amaryllis, would you? She's at Pamela Bowe's house."

"You're kidding!" I said. Amaryllis had never ventured into anyone's house before. Visiting was not in the books for us. Gypsies do not make a habit of visiting in other people's homes. Gypsies stuck to their own caravans. Gypsies were loose upon the world, but not loose upon other people's houses.

I clumped my way past orange lawn-and-leaf bags with jack-o'-lantern faces printed on them, smiling out from people's yards. I clumped my way past fences strung with lights that looked like tiny jack-o'-lanterns, glowing faintly orange in the late afternoon dimness. I clumped my way past miniature ghosts and goblins, being chaperoned by their moms and dads from door to door. I clumped my way to Pamela Bowe's house.

The trouble with Pamela Bowe's house was that it was guarded by vicious attack cats. Attack cats are much worse than attack dogs. Dogs might be mean, but they give you fair warning. They growl and rumble and drool and show their teeth and their entire selves. They are up front about the fact that they're going to rip you apart.

Attack cats aren't. They are clever and sneaky. They melt into sidewalks and bushes and brick steps. Then, when you least expect it, they fling themselves from their invisibility. They fly through the air, their claws extended like razors. They grab your unsuspecting legs and thighs, stabbing through the material of your clothing. They claw and scratch with abandon. Attack cats can give a person a heart attack.

I made my way to Pamela Bowe's front door, lurching right and left, trying to dodge the ambushes of her vicious cats. They flew at me from everywhere. Across the lawn, up the steps, from the very walls of the house they flew, howling and clawing! Out for blood!

By the time Pamela opened the front door, I was exhausted.

"I'm being attacked by your hordes of vicious cats!" I shrieked.

"My cats are not vicious, and we only have three," she retorted.

"Yeah, right," I said, dabbing at the bloody shreds of material my jeans had become.

"Your Aunt Sydney is right. You are melodramatic," said Pamela.

"She said that?" I asked. My Aunt Sydney did a lot of talking behind my back.

Pamela ignored me and led the way inside. I found Amaryllis and I told her she was wanted, and I walked her home. I didn't tell her about the letter. Maggie would want to do that. Besides, Amaryllis was in a mood. She dragged her feet and lagged behind.

"What's the matter with you these days?" I asked her.

She ignored me—a new Homer's Cove tradition.

By the time we got home, Harry's white pickup was parked behind my mother's yellow and green pickup.

When we walked in, Maggie, Harry, and Aunt Sydney were seated in the living room. The new old desk still sat in the same place, but the television behind it was silent. The whole room was silent. The whole house!

Maggie said softly to Amaryllis, "We need to talk, dear."

Amaryllis looked from her to Harry to Aunt Sydney. Then she looked at me.

I started to speak, but Maggie said to me, "You don't have to stay, Mackie."

"But you need me."

"No, it's okay I'm sure you have homework to do. Or something to do. Don't you, Mack?"

"It sounds as if you don't want me here."

"Maybe we should talk to Amaryllis alone," Maggie said.

"But he's here!" I shouted, pointing to Harry. "And she's here!" I shouted, pointing at Aunt Sydney.

"Mack, please," Maggie began, but I didn't wait for her to finish. I didn't have to be asked to leave twice. I knew when I wasn't wanted.

I stormed out of the house, slamming the front door so hard, the pumpkin lights that were strung around it rattled and shook.

I ran all the way down Maple Street, all the way down the Lake Shore Road, through Veteran's Park and down to the beach.

A huge lump blocked my throat. I couldn't swallow past it. I couldn't breathe. Then, suddenly, tears gushed out of my eyes like a waterfall. Before I knew it, I was sobbing. I ran across the beach to the dock. I threw myself onto the seat in the gazebo and poured my sorrow into the lake. At least the lake was always there, waiting patiently for me, listening to me.

The water of Lake George changed from summer to fall. During the summer, it was blue and glittery and inviting. In the fall, it was gray and shone as if oil had been spread over its choppy surface. The water of autumn looked exceedingly wet and cold.

Homer's Cove dock was lonely in the autumn. During the summer, the docks were busy with tourists in fancy boats with big motors. After summer was over and the tourists were gone, Homer's Cove people used the dock. Mostly, though, after the frost came, the dock was deserted.

Homer's Cove people's boats were not as fancy as the tourists' boats. They were "functional, not snazzy," as Harry said. Often, Homer's Cove people used canoes to get from one place to another on the lake.

Harry, who loved the lake and its stories, had explained to me, "That's how the Iroquois and the Algonquins got around—the good, old birch bark canoe. If it's good enough for them, it's good enough for us," he said.

"Then how come you use a motor boat?" I had asked him.

"Mack! Your mouth!" Maggie had said.

Harry just laughed and said, "Canoes don't pull water-skiers so well."

Harry loved to water-ski. He couldn't do it very much during the summer. He was busy at work, building docks and working on boathouses. And then, there was his antiques business, which is how he and Maggie met in the first place. But after Labor Day, Harry water-skied. The autumn was Harry's rest time, and the days usually stayed warm through most of October.

Harry took September and October for himself. It was after the tourist rush, but before Homer's Cove people pulled in their docks for the winter, so that the ice wouldn't wreck them. Or they put blowers under the docks. These blew big bubbles up, keeping ice from forming around the docks. Harry helped them do both things—docks and blowers.

"He's so handy!" Maggie would sigh.

When I had first seen the blowers at work, last winter down in Lake George Village I said, "It looks like King Neptune's sitting under the dock, blowing bubbles through a giant straw."

Aunt Sydney said, "King Neptune is found in the ocean, not in Lake George."

That spring, Amaryllis had had a funeral for King Neptune. She used an old Ken doll. She dressed him in a King Neptune toga. She put an old fork in his hand, to stand for Neptune's trident. He got buried between a Barbie and a goldfish.

That Halloween twilight, I sat sobbing in the gazebo by the lake. I quieted down eventually and listed my grievances to the lapping water. A lone canoe was docked close by, all but invisible in the dim light and the gray, choppy water.

A wind blew up, causing the waves in the water to rise. But the wind was not too cold; it was not a harsh wind. I looked out toward Dome Island. It sat in peace, like the dome of a turtle's shell or the hump of a camel, poking through the surface of Lake George. I remembered Cobb telling me about the skeleton of the cruise boat that had sunk off the shore of Dome Island.

I looked all around. Not a soul in sight.

"A quick canoe ride out to Dome Island wouldn't take too long," I reasoned to myself. I recalled the picture of Maggie, Amaryllis, Harry, and Aunt Sydney. In my mind, I remembered them all huddled together, apart from me, against me. "Besides, who would even notice I was gone? Who would even care?"

I tiptoed down to the canoe, as if anyone were close enough to hear me. As if anyone could hear me walk on sand. I surveyed the area. Nobody. The canoe might be docked for the entire night, abandoned, for all I knew.

"Well, why not?" I asked the waves.

"Who's to notice?" I asked the dock

"Who's to care?" I asked the wind.

"They're all too busy with themselves," I told the canoe, as I got in. I untied the line that held the canoe to the dock. It lurched out into the waves. The waves kicked up, lapping at the sides of the canoe.

"I'll go my way by myself," I sang out over the water. I pulled the oars through the waves, steering myself out toward Dome Island.

"I'll teach my heart how to sing!" The air was exhilarating! I felt free as the seagulls that screeched their way against the darkening sky.

"I'll go my way by myself, like a bird on the wing . . ."

I sang a song that rose from deep in my memory, a song that Maggie used to sing.

"I'll face the unknown!" I sang.

"I'll build a world all my own!

"No one knows better than I myself, I'm by myself, alone!"

I sang and shouted into the lake air, which grew colder and colder, the farther from shore I rowed. I pulled on the oars and plowed through the water, toward the ship's skeleton off Dome Island.

My arms burned and the muscles in them sang out in pain, even louder than I was singing. I could hardly hear my own song over the scream of the pain from my muscles! The cold waves chopped up around me. They threw the little canoe around, as if it were a banana peel. The air grew bitter. The light dimmed.

I remembered the stories I'd heard, sitting in Sheila's Diner. Or sitting on the stone wall in front of Ben & Jerry's, licking away at New York Super Fudge Chunk ice-cream cones. And I remembered stories Mrs. Keith had told me, while Maggie bought things from Mrs. Francis at Carroll's Department Store. I remembered stories Kee and Laurence told me, as they were sweeping the path to Finley's Fancy Restaurant.

Canoers often couldn't handle the rough waters of huge Lake George. People told stories of experienced canoers who were overturned by the winds that kicked up out of nowhere; canoers that were lost in the dense darkness that fell so quickly, once the sun went down, before the moon came up over the mountains. I recalled stories of canoes that were found adrift with no one in them and the reports of missing persons, which came in every autumn and of how, each spring, bodies of people who had been lost all winter would surface in the water behind Dottie's Restaurant, eleven miles down by Lake George Village. People that had been drowned in Northwest Bay, or by Dome Island, or right here at Homer's Cove. Bodies, bloated and with gray flesh hanging in shredded ribbons, having been nibbled by fish all winter, just bobbing up and down, up and down, behind Dottie's Restaurant. Would that be me?

Why hadn't I remembered any of these stories before I was so stupid as to take out this canoe? What made me think I could handle it? I was a tiny speck on a huge lake.

Would I ever see Kee and Laurence sweep their sidewalk again? Would I ever hear Mrs. Keith's stories? Would I ever lick Ben & Jerry's New York Super Fudge Chunk or dig into Sheila's monkey bread ever, ever again?

I fought the wind and the white-capped waves. The sun had dropped behind Black Mountain. It was dark and cold.

And my feet felt wet.

I tucked one oar under my arm and held it there tightly. If I lost an oar, I was surely lost. I bent down and, with my free hand, felt the bottom of the canoe.

Water.

There was a leak in the canoe!

Dome Island was a dim speck, far away in front of me. Homer's Cove was a dim speck, far away behind me. There were no other boaters about. Who would be dumb enough to boat on Halloween evening? Everybody else was in town trick-or-treating! Everybody *else* was gorging on Milky Ways and Starbursts! Only I was dumb enough to pull a stunt like this! I could just hear Aunt Sydney saying that exact thing to me, if . . . *if* . . . I ever got back home.

"Mack, you are a thorn in my side!" Aunt Sydney would say.

I wished I could hear her yell at me, right now. I wished I were home.

"Okay, God! I'll make a deal with you," I shouted

into the night. "You get me home, I will never, ever say a word against Aunt Sydney again, as long as I live. I will be the perfect niece to her, and the perfect daughter to Maggie, and the perfect sister to Amaryllis. I'll even call Maggie 'Mom'! And I'll be nice to Poppy and Daisy. I'll make friends! And You can even let them leave me—I won't mind! Just, please God, get me home!" I bargained.

"Okay, okay! That includes Harry, too. I'll even be nice to Harry," I pleaded. In the back of my mind, though, I reserved the thought, "Well, for a while, at least."

God must have heard my reserve thought and interpreted it as a cheat. Because he took away the last of the dim light and revved up the wind. God kicked up his heels, causing the waves to thrash about like madmen.

"I need balance. All I need is to balance this canoe," I advised myself. I took deep breaths. I pretended I was calm and mature. I pretended I was grown up. I pretended I was Harry.

"Harry would stay calm. Harry would not panic. Harry would keep himself afloat on the waves. That is what I will do. I will not panic and I will keep myself afloat on the waves. All night long."

In the dark, I could no longer see my feet. But I felt

the cold water prick at my ankles, over the rims of my sneakers.

I felt the waves splash water onto my wrists, over the sides of the canoe.

I felt the wind beat at my face. The wind which had turned bitter.

I felt what might be my last breath on earth.

Chapter 11

When there was a strong possibility that everything was going to be taken away from you, the way you looked at things changed. Things that upset you before, like flunking a math test, became not quite so upsetting. Things that were important to you before, like being able to beat Shadduck Fey at the hundred-yard dash, were not quite so important. Things that were horrible to you before, like having new people barge into your life, were not quite so horrible.

Things got juggled in your mind. Aunt Sydney's thorniness softened to the silky feel of a kitten's fur. Harry's smile was no longer sickeningly sweet; it was like a welcome sign shining from his face. Amaryllis's new friend Pamela Bowe might not be such an EWG. Her attack cats might not be quite so vicious.

"If only you get me home safe, God!" I was still bargaining.

How could you tell time, trapped in a boat in the middle of a dark lake? The sun had gone down. Behind Tongue Mountain, the dark sky showed a glow. I let the oars rest. The water jostled the canoe around.

But even in the middle of my terror, the glow behind Tongue Mountain was beautiful! The sky lit up in a white light. The moon rose majestically. It was a silver coin against a black velvet sky. It was a perfect hole letting the light of angels shine through.

"Is this the light at the end of the tunnel? Or is this the light that leads me to my death?" I thought of the stories on the TV talk shows, of people who said they died and came back to life. They saw a bright round light at the end of a tunnel.

Maybe this was not the moon rising behind Tongue Mountain. Maybe this was my bright light. Maybe this was my End.

The canoe was sinking. My legs were wet up to my shins. My arms ached. I panted in exhaustion. I knew the next wave would tip the canoe upside down! How could I fight the wind? How could I fight the water? Waves smashed sheets of water into my face. My hair was soaked. The wind ripped at it, slapping it back and forth against my face. The skin of my cheeks felt raw; my lips were puffed and cracked. The roar of the wind beat into my ears.

Maybe I should just give up! I thought, but pulled even harder at the oars. Giving up was not my cup of tea.

My lungs were ready to burst. I seemed to grow smaller and smaller, while the wind and the waves and the night grew bigger and bigger.

And then I heard, "Mack! Mackie!"

I spun around toward the voice. Was it God, calling me to my final reward? Would God call me Mackie?

I saw the red and green port and starboard lights of a boat charging through the water, directly toward me. The brilliant white light of a search light arced across the lake. It found me and settled on me like a morning star.

"There she is," I heard a voice over the roar of the wind and the waves and the boat engine.

"There she is!" The voice was familiar. It was Harry's voice! "Hold on, Mackie!" he shouted to me.

Finally, strong warm arms grabbed me and lifted me, cradled me.

Homer's Cove waited for me on the beach of Veterans Park-small-fry ghosts and goblins and witches and stuffed pumpkins, little hoboes and gypsies, with their mothers and fathers grasping their hands. As Harry carried me up from the dock, I saw the concerned faces of Mrs. Keith and Mrs. Francis, of Sheila, her husband, Ike, and Poppy and Daisy. Cobb was there, even more white and serious looking than usual, and so were Kee and Laurence. Then Homer's Cove became a blur and I didn't see any more faces, until I saw the face of the sun shining in through my bedroom window the next morning.

Aunt Sydney never called me a thorn in her side again. But Maggie did.

I stayed in the house, in my bathrobe, in constant sight of either Maggie, Aunt Sydney, or Amaryllis, for the next three days. I was not punished, though.

"You should punish her, you know," said Aunt Sydney.

"I am not the punishing type," said Maggie.

"Punishing is not her cup of tea," I said.

Aunt Sydney and Maggie gave me identical looks. I did not say anything more.

Mrs. Keith and Mrs. Francis stopped by to see me.

Mrs. Keith said, "You almost ended up behind Dottie's Restaurant!"

Mrs. Francis said, "Oh, dear!"

They brought me red and green plastic bangle bracelets.

"Think of Christmas, dear. It will cheer you up," said Mrs. Francis.

"Humpf! She should think of the port and starboard lights on the boat that saved her. Next time, she might not be so lucky," huffed Mrs. Keith.

Sheila and her sister stopped by. Ms. Marmalyde brought me a library copy of *Peggy Lee and the Mysterious Islands.*

"I think this book is right up your alley, Mack," she whispered.

Sheila brought me my own mound of monkey bread.

"You don't have to share it with anyone," she smiled. She added, "Poppy and Daisy are outside. They'd love to see you. Do you feel up to it?"

It was time for me to make a big decision. Yes, I remembered my promise to God. But no, I did not feel ready to start any friendship that would end up in my being deserted once again.

God won out.

I nodded and smiled shyly. I did not know what to expect. As far as I knew, Poppy and Daisy hated me. Who could blame them, the way I'd acted?

The door opened and their two heads peeked in, Poppy's on top, Daisy's lower. I gulped, called up my courage, and smiled. They became brave when they saw my smile and came all the way into the room. They tiptoed over to the bed, stuck together side by side as if they dared not separate from each other, for fear I'd attack.

"Well. Hey," I tried.

"Hey!" they tried together. Poppy tilted her head.

"Um," I tried again.

"Um," they tried together.

Then Poppy said, "That musta been real scary out there."

"Well, a little, maybe," I shrugged.

With that, Daisy came over to the bed and put her hand flat onto the pillow. "Poppy and I think you're real brave, Mack."

"Really?" I asked, pleased.

"Yeah. Brave," said Daisy.

"But dumb," said Poppy.

I looked at them. "You know what? I agree. You are absolutely right. I am brave but dumb!"

We laughed together. They asked if they could come back the next day and practice music with me.

"You play flute, I play clarinet, and Poppy plays French horn. We might sound good together," said Daisy, grinning brightly.

I wasn't so sure about the way we might sound, and I wasn't absolutely positive that I wanted any friends, but I said, "Great!" anyway.

After they left, I looked up to where I figured God was and whispered to him, "Maybe You're right after all." Then, as a way of telling Him He hadn't won me over completely yet, I added, *"Maybe."*

Kee and Laurence sent me a card that said on the cover, "I know things have been pretty tough . . ." and then on the inside, "But every beautiful flower has to go through lots of dirt to blossom. Good luck." It was attached to a pot of bright red geraniums.

Cobb came by and said, "You want to see the boat's skeleton so bad, you should have asked me to take you."

"That wasn't really the point," I told him, thinking him a little dull witted not to realize my canoe ride was more than just a sightseeing trip.

"Well, see any bass while you were out there?" he asked.

I played my flute a lot during those days at home. The music of the flute was like a cocoon for me. I felt I could crawl in and nourish myself. I had always felt that way about my music. I practiced scales and a Debussy piece called "Syrinx." The sheet music cover said *"pour flute seul"*—alone, solo—that was definitely me. "Syrinx" had a sad, lonely sound. I wallowed in it. I was not up to playing my favorite John Philip Sousa marches. I saved them for when I was feeling cheerful, not down in the dumps as I was feeling so often these days.

I was in the middle of a trill when my bedroom door popped open. It was Maggie.

"Shadduck Fey's downstairs. He'd like to visit," she announced.

I tried to get Maggie to turn him away at the door.

"Do you want me to get sicker?" I asked her.

"You're not sick," she said, dryly.

"Do you want me to get sick?" I asked her.

"Mack, you are a thorn in my side," she said.

"Good grief," I said.

"You act like a nut, Mack Humbel," Shadduck Fey said when Maggie escorted him into my room.

He brought me a strange object. It was like a little tube. It was made of a brownish, swirly plastic kind of material. When you held it up to the light, you could see through it. It cast a reddish-brown glow on your face, when you held it up. One end was narrow, like a straw. The other end was wide and had a gold rim around it.

"That's real gold!" said Shadduck.

It came in a leather case. The leather was beaten and battered.

"What is this?" I asked Shadduck.

"It's a cigar holder. It's real old. My uncle said it's from England."

Maggie looked at it. "Why, Shadduck, it's wonderful! It must be seventy or eighty years old!" she exclaimed.

"It's a antique!" Shadduck exclaimed.

"*An* antique, you mean," I corrected him.

Maggie laughed and told me I sounded like Aunt Sydney. Then she said, "I am mesmerized by this, Shadduck. Where *do* you get these interesting things?"

Shadduck Fey lit up like a tree at Christmas. "My uncle. He collects weird things."

"Does he know you have this?" asked Maggie.

Here was my chance. Maybe Shadduck would be arrested for thievery and put into jail!

"He lets me buy things from him. I work for them. I'm going to shovel his sidewalk for the first four snowstorms for this." Shadduck looked at Maggie and his face beamed with pride. He added, "And let me tell you, snowstorms around here have lots and lots of snow to them!"

"Well, you are a hard worker, Shadduck," said Maggie, kindly.

Shadduck Fey beamed some more.

"So who around here smokes cigars, anyway? You think I look like a cigar smoker?" I asked Shadduck.

"That's not the point, Mack. It's a lovely gift. Whether or not we are cigar smokers is simply not the point," said Maggie, reminding me of what I had said to Cobb when he talked to me about my canoe trip to Dome Island. Reminding me that I had thought Cobb a little obtuse, not understanding why I'd taken the canoe. Maggie must have thought me just as obtuse, just as dense.

"The rim's real gold. That's the point, Mack Humbel," gloated Shadduck Fey. "Ahem!" he cleared his throat, then said, "It's a gold ring!" He looked at me like a sick puppy.

Words failed me. I rolled my eyes, Amaryllis-like. First the kiss, now the gold ring. I felt a stirring in my veins. I knew exactly what it was.

"Maggie, it is definitely time to move," I said.

On the Monday after Halloween, as I was dressing for school, Maggie knocked on my door.

"Where's Amaryllis?" she asked.

"In the bathroom."

"Well, we're taking her in to school today. We have an appointment with her teacher and the principal."

"We do?"

"Well, Harry and I, that is," Maggie said.

"Oh," I said.

"Has Amaryllis mentioned anything to you about it?" Maggie asked. Maggie was still under the impression that Amaryllis talked to me. It was an impression I used to like to give, but not anymore, now it was scaring me.

"Um. No. Not in so many words," I said.

"Well, in what words?" Maggie asked.

"Well, in no words," I said.

"What do you mean, Mack?"

"Amaryllis doesn't exactly talk to me. In words, that is," I stammered.

Maggie didn't say anything. She folded her arms and looked at me, frowning. The sun shone in on her hair, sparking it with gold and copper. She wore a rust-colored blouse, with pants to match. She looked like a warm flame. A worried, warm flame.

"Did she ever speak to you? Since the fire, I mean. Since your Dad . . . ?" Maggie asked me in a quiet voice.

"Well . . ."

"The truth, Mack."

"Well, no, Mom," I said.

"I thought so."

"It just made me feel better to pretend," I whispered.

"I understand. It made me feel better to pretend, too. But I knew, in back of my mind, she was not speaking even to you, Mack. Pretending is sometimes a comfort. However, this is real. When it begins to interfere with school, and with our lives, it gets real. Amaryllis's teacher is worried. I guess we haven't been in one school long enough for them to pick up on the extent of the problem. I guess Homer's Cove School is special. It pays attention to its students," Maggie said.

"But this isn't such a big problem that we can't deal with it, is it, Mom?" I asked.

Amaryllis had come into the room. She was all ears. She looked at me and then at Maggie and then at me again. Her eyes were dark today, and wide.

Maggie smiled. "Reverting back to Mom, hey?" She

came over and gave me a hug. Amaryllis joined us in the hug. We huddled together.

"Sometimes problems have a way of making us feel very young and small, don't they?"

I nodded, my face tucked into my mother's neck. I heard the rustle of Maggie's blouse, as Amaryllis nestled into our mother's neck, on the other side.

"Of course, we can deal with it, my girls. We always have, haven't we? Uh-oh, is that Harry's truck I hear?" She ran to the window.

"Yes, it is," she said. "Amaryllis, you ready?"

Amaryllis nodded and followed her down the stairs.

I didn't want to go to school that day. I wanted to stay home and dust with Aunt Sydney. I wanted to watch talk shows on TV and make hot chocolate with marshmallows and eat the rest of the monkey bread Sheila had brought me.

But I went to school, and I watched the hands of the clock drag themselves, minute by minute, from eight-thirty to two-thirty. Then the bell rang and I ran home, to learn of what had happened at the meeting that would decide Amaryllis's fate.

Chapter 12

M iss Ponfret was Amaryllis's teacher. She was as thin as Ms. Marmalyde was round. Her hair was as brown and mousy as Ms. Marmalyde's was bright and brassy. She was as cold as Ms. Marmalyde was warm.

Miss Ponfret said to Maggie, "If your daughter does not start communicating with us, I have no choice but to refer her to an alternate educational program."

Mr. Grim, the principal, straightened his black bow tie and said, "We'd like to do testing to see if there's something, well, wrong with Amaryllis. Then we can design a learning program specifically for her."

"You're talking about a special classroom, for children with severe problems. You can't label Amaryllis that way! She doesn't deserve it; she doesn't need it! Her grades are fine. Her behavior is exemplary!" said Maggie, with great force.

"Special Education is not a label. And I certainly can do whatever I see fit for my students!" countered Miss Ponfret, turning red and agitated.

Mr. Grim held out his hands in stop signals. He said, "Now, now, ladies. Mrs. Humbel, there is no shame in having a child in Special Education. If a child is classified, it simply means that child needs a little extra help."

Maggie didn't let him get any further. "A label is a label, Mr. Grim. My girls will not be labeled! Period! If I have anything to say about it."

Miss Ponfret calmed down. She said in kindness, "You know, we are aware that Amaryllis's father passed away. Was it from illness?"

"No. He was killed in a fire. He was a fireman. He was saving his family. And he was killed," Maggie told her quietly, folding her hands in her lap.

"That could very well be the source of Amaryllis's problem," said Ms. Ponfret.

"We believe it is," agreed Maggie.

"We care about our children here in Homer's Cove, Mrs. Humbel. We like to treat our students as individual people with individual needs and preferences, not as lumps of brains coming to school to learn how to add and how to spell," said Mr. Grim.

"I respect that. But I will not allow my daughter to be taken out of her regular classroom," said Maggie.

Mr. Grim sighed. Miss Ponfret sighed. Maggie sighed. Harry shifted in his seat.

Then Miss Ponfret rallied. "But I do insist, if Amaryllis does not start communicating, that she be tested and most likely sent to the special school down in Fort Edward. It is a school with teachers that handle such problems."

Harry filled me in on all that had gone on in the meeting.

"Your mom was strong, Mackie. She was something else."

"Well, I couldn't have done it if you hadn't been there, Harry. Just having your support, it let me be strong," said Maggie.

"Does this mean they're not going to let me and Amaryllis go to the same school? They're going to send her everyday, all the way down to Fort Edward? She'll have to leave before the sun comes up! She won't get home until nighttime!"

Maggie took Harry's hand and held it so tightly, her knuckles turned white. "If Amaryllis doesn't begin communicating, that's what will happen." Maggie's eyes glistened with tears. One little one escaped and rolled down her cheek. Harry caught it with his finger. He pulled her close.

"What about the guidance counselor?" asked Aunt Sydney. "I told you to schedule her with the guidance counselor, at least once a week. That's the least that school can do!"

"Amaryllis will see the school counselor twice a week. Don't worry, Sydney," said Harry. Maggie had shrunk into herself.

"Sure! If they remember! If they can fit her in! I know these schools!" snorted Aunt Sydney.

Amaryllis crept into the living room and snuggled onto the couch, between Harry and Maggie. She "ritched" and "rootched" until she'd buried herself into the cushions. She looked with serious eyes at Maggie.

I bit my thumb, watching the three of them. Aunt Sydney walked behind the couch and stood above them. It was a family portrait, and I wasn't in it.

I said, "I've said it before and I'll say it again. It's time to move!"

They stood there and stared, remaining in their family portrait. I got the distinct feeling that I was talking to a stone wall.

The doorbell rang. I saw Pamela Bowe's face peeking through the window in the door. Amaryllis jumped up from between Maggie and Harry, grabbed her jacket, waved to us all, and left, arm in arm with Pamela Bowe.

"That was a quick change of mood," commented Aunt Sydney.

Harry said, "Pamela might be just what that little girl needs."

"What that little girl needs is to be left alone. What that little girl needs is a new town where they mind their own business. What that little girl needs is ME!" I shouted.

Maggie looked at Harry, Aunt Sydney looked at Maggie, Harry looked at me. I looked at the camel, then at the memory jug. I bolted out of the chair and shot up the stairs to my room. I went to Amaryllis's dresser and picked up one of her pink plastic barrettes. She used to wear them, to keep her hair out of her face. But now, she braided her hair in one braid down her back. Like Pamela Bowe.

I took the barrette, leaned under the bed, and drew out my Special Things Shoe Box. I opened it and set the barrette in it gently. I sat down on my bed. It made a comfortable, familiar squeak. One by one, I picked up the things in my Special Things Shoe Box. I remembered each memory that each thing represented.

I fondled the hero's medal Daddy had received.

"You're my hero for always, Daddy," I prayed to him. I thought, I need to work harder to keep our little family together, the way it was, for Daddy's sake.

I held the first antique thing that Maggie ever gave me. It was a tiny Christmas elf, made of chalk. It's red paint was worn to pink, and its white beard was chipped. It was sitting with one leg bent under it, the other leg extended.

"Your grandma used to bring this out every Christmas. She put it on the piano, along with the iron reindeer she used to collect," Maggie told me.

I lifted out a tiny plastic bracelet that said HUMBEL, BABY, F. It was the bracelet the hospital put on my ankle when I was born. The "Baby" meant I was a newborn. The "F" meant I was a female.

When I had first shown it to a four-and-a-half-year-old Amaryllis, she had said, "Mine!" It was one of the last times she ever spoke.

"No. Mine!" I snapped at her. Maybe I shouldn't have snapped at Amaryllis so much when we were kids. Maybe she'd be normal today. But down deep I knew it wasn't me that put my sister into her silence. It was the fire. It was what happened to Daddy. We had asked him to save Lorraine. We had killed him. It was our fault. And Amaryllis just could not handle knowing that. Not the way I could.

"Hey, Mackie," said Harry.

I looked out of the corner of my eyes at him.

"Maggie said maybe I could come up and talk to you," he said gently. He pulled a chair over (one of Maggie's uncomfortable ballroom chairs that girls were not supposed to sit on, because it meant they were duds at dances) and sat down, facing me. Harry was so big and solid, he made the chair look like dollhouse furniture.

I bent my head down, pretending to look deeply into my Special Things Shoe Box.

"Amaryllis is growing up, isn't she, Mackie?"

"Yep," I said curtly.

"We all do, don't we, Mackie?"

179

"Yep."

"And things are always changing, aren't they?"

"Yep."

"Hard to take, sometimes, isn't it?"

I gulped. My eyes stung with tiny pinpricks. I couldn't say yep again. The word stuck in my throat.

"Sometimes we have to grin and bear it. And sometimes we have to take the bull by the horns and do something about it. What do you think you're going to do?" Harry asked me. I had never heard him so serious.

"What do you mean?" I asked.

"I mean about Amaryllis. You have two choices as to what to do. You can put up with it, and maybe get an ulcer by the time you're fourteen, or you can take the bull by the horns and do something about it. What are you going to do, Mackie?"

"Move."

Harry picked up his chair and scooched it over toward the door a couple of inches.

I sucked my teeth. "Tsssk!" I said. "I don't mean you move. I mean us. We should move again. To someplace where they don't get so personal."

"One time, after you first moved here, Maggie told me that Sydney said to her, 'You can't run from pain. You have to face it to get through it.' She was right, Mack. Pain has a way of getting fat and heavy if people run away from it."

Harry put his hands on his knees. He leaned over and peered into my Special Things Shoe Box.

"Can I have a look?" he asked.

I shoved the box at him. He took it. His big, thick fingers moved through the mementos in my box gently, more so than I could ever have imagined.

"You know what this reminds me of, Mackie? It reminds me of my memory jug, downstairs," Harry said.

"Yeah, so?"

"So, how about we make a memory jug? For you? For all your memories?"

"I asked Maggie once. She said no."

"She did?"

"She did."

"Well, maybe I could talk to her. Maybe I could . . ."

"No, thanks. You've done enough," I told Harry. I got up off the bed and flounced past him, trying to look sophisticated and dramatic. I tripped over his feet and fell flat on my face. Rarely could I make a grand and gracious exit. I jumped up and ran down the stairs and out the backdoor.

Harry and Maggie called, "Mack! Mack Humbel, come back here!"

Too late! I was on the run once again. I was getting used to it.

I ran down Maple Street, around the corner by the school and up Horicon, way, way up to where the houses stopped and big boulders lined the roadway. I scaled up one of them and sat atop it. I panted, my lungs ready to burst.

Up here, you could see all of Homer's Cove and you could look out onto Lake George. You could see the white ship shape of the Northwind Hotel jutting out into the gray waters of the November lake.

I cooled down from my run quickly. At first, the cold wind felt good. I had been sweating under my sweater and the wool itched. But then the wind blew icier and made me shiver.

I was strong, though. As strong as Maggie. I would face the wind. I would shiver in silence.

The sun settled behind Black Mountain, and the streetlights of Homer's Cove twinkled on, scattering down the Lake Shore Road. The Northwind lights lit up the lake, reflecting on it so that there were two hotels, one upside down, for the lake creatures to enjoy, and one right side up, for the humans to have.

The world was the color of a young robin's feathers. The amber glow of lamps from people's homes dotted on, one by one, throughout the village. Homer's Cove invited me to come back down and to nestle into it. Homer's Cove invited me in for a warm cup of hot chocolate and the sweet taste of monkey bread.

I shivered some more, got up from the rock, and climbed down. I walked slowly home, thinking of Amaryllis. I had to make her talk. I had to save her from being sent away to another school. I had to save her from more psychiatrists. I had to keep us all together.

I had to save the day for the Humbel family in Homer's Cove.

Chapter 13

All through the rest of autumn, through midterms and the Homer's Cove Talent Show, through Thanksgiving turkey and after-Thanksgiving leftovers, through band practices and the first snow, I stuck to my sister like flypaper, like Scotch tape, like glue.

One day after the last bell in school, Shadduck Fey asked me, "What do you think you're doing? You're going to drive your sister nuts."

"It's for her own good. I'm sticking to her like glue."

"Yea, crazy glue. Hey, did you know they invented crazy glue to glue shot-up soldiers back together, in the war?" Shadduck not only had lots of weird objects, he also had weird information.

"Huh?"

"Only it didn't work. So they just let regular people use it. But not on each other."

"Um. Right. Well, I've got to go get Amaryllis now. So long," I said, making a quick getaway out the school doors. I tracked down my sister, who was walking home alone.

"Hey, wait up!" I called.

Amaryllis looked behind her, spotted me, turned away, and walked on, faster and faster. Her skinny legs churned like the propellers of a boat.

"Hey, wait up!" I called again, as if I thought she hadn't heard me; as if I thought she hadn't seen me. Amaryllis was not drifting away from me; she was charging away full steam ahead.

On days when Amaryllis walked home with Pamela Bowe, it had become a routine for me to tag closely behind. They would walk in silence. I would chatter. They were still quiet; I was still a squirrel.

Day after day, I braved Pamela's attack cats when we went into her house for chips and soda after school. I endured her thin stare when we went to Cobb's Hardware to check out his prices on Christmas lights for Maggie. I even let her intrude on our trips to Sheila's for monkey bread.

"Well, the three musketeers, once again!" Sheila would say.

Amaryllis and Pamela would smile widely. I would sink my head into my shoulders like a turtle.

But at least we were together, Amaryllis and me. I had become her right hand, her idea man, her advisory board. And I advised her, every step of the way. It was important that I counsel Amaryllis and make her normal, so she would not be sent away to Fort Edward, to the special class.

I recommended what clothes she should wear in the morning and what way she should walk home in order to avoid Shadduck Fey, or to avoid the snowball army of boys, when the snows came to Homer's Cove. I changed the channels for her on TV, because I knew what shows she liked. I sang songs to her when we were lying in our beds going to sleep at night. I was taking exemplary care of my sister, as Maggie would have said.

But Amaryllis became increasingly difficult to care for. When I laid out her clothes in the morning, she often threw them on the floor, kicked them under her bed, and then dressed in ugly stuff that an EWG would wear.

One Saturday afternoon, I walked into the living room and found her staring at the TV, which was not even on. I picked up the clicker and turned the television on for her. I clicked through until I got to Nickelodeon, which was the very thing I knew she would enjoy.

"This is what you want to watch," I told her.

She grabbed the clicker from me, jammed it in the direction of the television, and clicked the set off. She looked at me with a fierce expression burning in her eyes.

I grabbed the clicker back from her and clicked the TV back on.

She jumped up and tore the clicker from my hand. She clicked the TV off again. I tried to wrench the clicker out of her grip. She wrestled me to the ground. I humpfed and ground my teeth and yelled, "Hey! Hey!"

I thought I heard Amaryllis humpf. I thought I heard Amaryllis murmur. But it was probably the blood rushing to my brain, because she had me upside down and in a crunch.

I managed to get the clicker from her, but she wrestled it back out of my hand, pushed me unceremoniously over and into the legs of the collection of antique footstools that still surrounded the chair, and jumped up. She ran to the window, opened it wide, and threw the clicker outside with all her might.

She turned to me, pulled herself up tall (much as Aunt Sydney would have done), gave a distinct *Humpf!*, and left the room.

Amaryllis had made a sound. Or, at least, I *thought* so. But at the same time I thought, I am losing my sister.

"Pamela Bowe is a terrible influence on Amaryllis," I told Maggie later that evening, while I was wiping the supper dishes she was washing.

"Pamela Bowe is a good influence on Amaryllis," she said, simply.

"Harry is a terrible influence on Amaryllis," I replied.

"Harry is a good influence on Amaryllis," she said, simply.

"Aunt Sydney is . . ." I began, but Maggie turned to face me squarely, put her fists on her hips, stuck her tongue in her cheek, placed her feet solidly on the floor, as if getting ready for a boxing round, and gave me one of her looks.

"I'm waiting," she said.

I said nothing.

"I'm waiting," she repeated.

"What are we waiting for?" asked Aunt Sydney, who

walked into the kitchen with Harry. "Here's a couple more coffee cups for the washup crew," she said. "What are we waiting for?"

"The city bus," I retorted crisply, and stalked out of the kitchen. I hissed to myself, "Grown-ups! They just don't understand!"

I refused to let Amaryllis's attitude interfere with my keeping a close eye on her. We all go through stages of rebellion, I reasoned to myself. I heard about that on enough TV talk shows. I simply had to work my way through her moods and get her to talk. I would not let my sister get labeled in Fort Edward.

Whenever I could tear Amaryllis away from Pamela Bowe, I would take her up Horicon hill, up past where the houses ended, to the boulders that lined the road.

Harry told us that there were glaciers, eons ago. When the glaciers melted, they chiseled out these huge rocks. The glaciers were so massive, they tossed the boulders around as if they were Nerf balls. A long time ago, men carved a road out of the boulders. Horicon Avenue. Now, the big rocks sat guarding both sides of the road.

Trout Creek ran up on the hill, behind the boulders that lined Horicon. When there was lots of rain, the creek swelled and water seeped through the boulders, cascading down them and across the road. In cold weather, black ice would form. It was invisible, and people traveling Horicon had to be careful. Black ice often covered the Northway, too, and people driving down the big expressway had had bad accidents.

When we returned to school after Thanksgiving vacation, Mr. Platte told us, "Winter in the Adirondacks is beautiful, but it can be treacherous, too. You have to be careful, in the Adirondacks in the winter."

"It's full of danger!" I said.

"Full of danger!" he agreed.

"That's why we have to keep eating Sheila's monkey bread. So we can be full of energy, to fight the danger!" I laughed. "C'mon, Amaryllis, let's go get some monkey bread," I said, tugging at her arm.

Mr. Platte called to me, "Hang on. Here comes Pamela."

Good grief.

Amaryllis stopped. She stared at me.

"What's the matter with you? Don't you want monkey bread?" I asked her.

She shook her head. No.

"You're not getting tired of it, are you?" I asked her.

She shrugged her shoulders. Maybe.

"Are you getting tired of monkey bread or aren't you?" I was getting angry. People kept changing things around on me.

She nodded. Yes.

"Well, let's go do something else," I said.

Amaryllis turned her back to me. She sucked her teeth, *tssking* loudly, and marched away. Pamela marched right after her.

What did Amaryllis see in Pamela that she couldn't find in her own sister? I didn't remember ever feeling so alone.

Poppy and Daisy came up by my side.

"What's with that sister of mine?" I asked no one in particular.

"She has other fish to fry," Poppy said.

"What fish does she have to fry, without me?"

"She does have a life, you know," said Daisy.

I backed away from her. "No, she doesn't!" I said.

"Yes, she does," she said.

"Y' know, you are not my cup of tea!" I yelled.

"And you're not mine, either!" she yelled back.

Poppy and Daisy turned away from me and I turned away from them. We each walked a few steps in opposite directions, as if we were going to fight a duel. Then we all, as one, hesitated and turned back around.

I asked in a whisper, "So, you want to go to Sheila's?" I almost swallowed the question; I was unsure I wanted them to hear. I could not handle another rejection.

Daisy shrugged her dainty shoulders. "I suppose," she whispered back.

Poppy's head nodded in agreement. Then she tilted her left ear to her left shoulder and smiled a tentative smile.

We walked to Sheila's slowly and in silence, testing the waters, walking on eggs!

The monkey bread was not quite so good that day.

"Maybe you should try something new," advised Sheila.

"I think I am," I said, looking at Poppy and Daisy, up to their wrists in monkey bread.

By the time I got back home, I found Maggie and Aunt Sydney in the backyard with Amaryllis. They were all dressed for a funeral. They were waiting for me.

"Who died this time?" I asked.

Amaryllis held out a milk carton for me to examine. She had cut one side off of it and held it on the other side, so the open side was to the top. Inside lay a Raggedy Ann with no head and a torn dress.

"Boy, that's an old doll. I thought we already buried this one," I said.

"Obviously not," Aunt Sydney said.

"Will you say a few words, Mack?" Maggie said.

"Maybe I should get my flute," I offered.

"Just a few words, Mack," said Aunt Sydney, obviously anxious to get through this as quickly as possible.

I walked up to the head of the hole Amaryllis had dug in the snow-dusted yard. I cleared my throat.

"We are gathered here for yet another funeral . . ." I started. I motioned to Amaryllis, who was still holding the milk carton coffin. "You're supposed to put the coffin in the grave, now," I said.

I started again, "We are gathered here for yet another . . ."

Amaryllis continued to stand, holding the coffin.

"Amaryllis, NOW, please," I said, holding to my official capacity as funeral director.

Amaryllis stiffened; her legs became poles of steel, her arms clasped the coffin to her chest like iron clamps. Her head sat stiffly on a neck as rigid as a lamppost.

"PUT THE COFFIN IN THE GRAVE!" I demanded.

Amaryllis, still clutching the coffin to her heart, started zooming around the yard. She tore around the border of the yard again and again. The black veils she had put on for the funeral streamed out behind her. She opened her mouth wide, in a silent scream. She shut her eyes tight, darting around by memory and by luck so that she wouldn't run into a tree.

Maggie and Aunt Sydney stood by the open grave and turned and turned, following Amaryllis with their eyes, not knowing what to do. Their mouths hung open, shooting out frosted question-mark plumes of breath. I did the same.

Finally, Amaryllis ran right up at me, came to a screeching halt about an inch away from me, took the coffin with Raggedy still in it, and beat me over the head with it.

"Hey!" I yelled, trying to rub my head, back up, and grab the coffin from her, all at the same time.

She kept pummeling me with it. She grunted and spat. Her veils and her hair flew around her head. She was sweating and panting.

"Hey!" I screamed again, holding up my arms as a shield from the pounding coffin.

She stamped her feet on the ground, right, left, right, left, in a fit. She continued to pummel and to stamp her feet. Then she opened her mouth wide, took in a great, deep breath, and screamed, "Mack Humbel! Mack Humbel! Mack Humbel! You are so, SO, SO OVER-BEARING!"

Aunt Sydney said, "You know, I must agree with her."

Maggie said, "Don't be rude, Amaryllis."

I yelled, "But you're *supposed* to . . ."

We stopped. We looked at Amaryllis.

She stood there, tears streaming down her red cheeks, her chest heaving. Her breath came out in loud sobs. Her coffin was in shreds, and so was Raggedy.

Amaryllis's tears were contagious, because, all at once, we were crying and yammering. We lunged at Amaryllis as if she were a falling star from heaven that might disappear. We hugged her and kissed her. We hugged each other and kissed each other.

Suddenly, Maggie and I and Aunt Sydney became as silent as stone. We stepped away from Amaryllis, staring at her. One question was on all of our minds.

Will she talk again?

Amaryllis continued to stand, looking down into her wrecked coffin. She sniffled mightily, wiping her nose with her pink-mittened hand.

She looked at me and said, "You're . . . so . . . very . . . bossy."

"I . . . I . . . ," I said. "I . . . I . . . I . . . . I . . . ."

"I think Raggedy isn't quite dead yet. I think I need to operate. Yes, I've definitely decided to save her life," said my sister. She spoke slowly, concentrating on every word, nodding her head slowly up and down.

"Okay," I said.

"That sounds like a marvelous idea," Aunt Sydney said in a breathy voice, as if she were afraid talking too loud might burst the magic bubble we soared in.

"That sounds like we should celebrate. Hot chocolate, anyone?" Maggie said in words that sounded as if they had fought their way directly from her heart, out past a lump of tears that had collected in her throat.

"With marshmallows!" I said, my own voice all choked up.

"Double marshmallows," Maggie said.

"And you can have mine, if you want them," I offered.

"I just want my own," my sister said sharply.

"That's okay, too," Aunt Sydney said.

We walked together back into our home, its amber glow shining out into the winter air, making a golden path in the snowy yard. As we made our little procession, snowflakes sifted down from the darkening sky. They glistened like diamonds on our hair and our eyelashes.

We four females in the snow tilted our faces upward and opened our mouths. Snowflakes fell on our tongues, feeling cold and clean. We walked through the door of our little nest, and closed it firmly behind us.

Through the snowy weeks toward Christmas, Amaryllis spoke erratically. Days went by when she just smiled and shrugged and nodded, like before. Fear seized each of us. Would she talk again? And then, in spurts, she would blabber on until she was blue in the face.

Harry said, "I'm really getting a kick out of your sister, Mack."

Harry was getting a kick out of everything, this time of year.

"You know what's coming up, don't you?" he asked me.

"Christmas, Harry," I said patiently, humoring him.

"More than Christmas, Mackie, more than Christmas," he said, mysteriously.

He took me to Carrol's Department Store, looking for Christmas presents. I went directly to the counter with the piles and ropes and mounds of jewelry, its silver and gold and bright reds and blues, and its diamonds and ruby and emerald-colored glass sparkling and twinkling. I stood a long time in front of the counter.

"Is that supposed to be a hint?" Harry asked me, laughing softly.

"Getting ready for your Christmas boat ride, Mr. Goodwell?" asked Mrs. Keith.

"Oh, dear," said Mrs. Francis. "Again?"

"Every year!" said Harry. He grinned at them. They did not grin back.

"You are risking your life, Harry Goodwell. Do you want to come bobbing up behind Dottie's Restaurant next spring?" asked Mrs. Keith.

"The youngsters say, 'Go to Dottie's for Bodies!' you know, Mr. Goodwell!" said Mrs. Francis, with great feeling, nodding her head up and down in short jerks, so that her gray curls shook.

"Never fear, ladies. My Christmas tradition is perfectly safe, and the event of the winter!"

"Um, Harry, isn't it kind of cold to take a boat ride on Christmas Day?" I asked.

"And that's not the half of it!" said Mrs. Keith.

"Not the half," agreed Mrs. Francis.

Mrs. Keith leaned over the counter. She stuck her face into mine, frowned fiercely and hissed, "He water-skis!"

"Water-skis?"

"Water-skis! On Christmas Day!" She breathed a deep *humpff* and pulled herself to her greatest height.

Mrs. Francis nodded her head vigorously. "Water-skis! Oh, dear!"

Harry laughed, paid for his purchase for Maggie, which was a red baseball cap to match his own. He put his arm around my shoulders and led me out the door.

"It's a tradition, y'know. A Homer's Cove–Harry Goodwell tradition. I haven't missed a Christmas Day boat ride in eight years. And your mom promised you'd all be joining me this year."

"Out on the lake? It's too cold!"

"Nope. You'll love it. Lots of people come to watch."

"You aren't going to make us all water-ski, are you?" I asked, gulping.

Harry smiled. "No, no, Mackie Humbel. Fear not. Harry Goodwell will keep you safe and warm, and never, ever force you to water-ski on Christmas Day. Unless you want to," he added, his eyes twinkling.

"Good grief," I said.

"Good golly," he answered.

"Good grief," I repeated.

Chapter 14

Aunt Sydney tore through the house as she'd never torn through the house before.

"Our first Christmas in Homer's Cove. Our first Christmas in our home!" she sang among the few errant cobwebs she could find, tucked away in dark corners.

"Sounds as if you're planning on staying forever. In somebody else's home," I said to my aunt.

"One never knows, one never knows," she sang.

"Well, don't bank on it," I said.

"Don't bank on what?" Maggie asked.

"One never knows, one never knows," I sang.

Maggie and I sang Christmas songs, with Amaryllis joining in on only an end word here and there, and always off by a beat.

"Dashing through the snow . . ." sang Maggie and I.

" . . . snow," sang Amaryllis, a moment late.

"In a one-horse open sleigh . . ."

" . . . sleigh."

"O'er the fields we go . . ."

" . . . go."

"Laughing all the way . . ."

Nothing.

Maggie and I sang again, "Laughing all the way . . ."

Again, nothing.

Aunt Sydney said, "You can't expect perfection."

Amaryllis smiled at her.

The snow started falling in serious squalls two weeks before Christmas. The snowbanks grew, towering over the tops of cars parked along the street, towering over the heads of schoolchildren as they made their way through white tunnels to school each morning. The temperature never fell too far below twenty-eight degrees, so it never got cold enough for the lake to freeze. Harry watched the thermometer every day.

"I can't water-ski through fourteen-inch ice," Harry

said. "Usually the lake doesn't freeze till late January, but you never know," he said with a worried look on his face.

This winter, Homer's Cove turned into a perfect crystal palace of snow, set alongside an unfrozen lake. Everybody was happy.

The Lake Shore Road was a Christmas fairyland. When you were in a car, driving up from Lake George Village, the first place you saw was the big Payle mansion. Mr. Payle and his family owned many factories that made pots and pans. They had been selling Payle's Pots and Pans for years and years. They were very rich. In fact, Mr. Payle was so rich that when his grandchildren came to visit and proved too noisy, he built them their own mansion. It was big and white and tucked into the shoreline right alongside his stone mansion. It had its own servants and its own boathouse.

Even though Mr. Payle didn't seem very nice about his grandchildren, he was very nice about decorating both his mansions for Christmas. They were strung all over with Christmas lights of many colors. Along the snow-covered stone walls and iron fences that surrounded the mansions, lights reflected in reds and greens and yellows and blues. They shone through the fluffy white covering of snow, looking like colored stars shining through angel wings.

On each side of the iron gate entrance, there were two stone columns with a great stone ball atop each. Mr. Payle had these wrapped in red foil, with evergreen garlands and colored lights strung around them.

Even the fancy white boathouse of the children's mansion was lit by strings of colored lights. A Christmas tree stood on the boathouse deck.

The Payle mansions were the last colored lights you saw as you entered Homer's Cove. All the rest were white fairy lights.

Tavern on the Creek was a little outside of the main clump of business buildings in Homer's Cove, and it was kind of new, so people didn't really count it with the regular business in the heart of Homer's Cove. But the tavern marked the entryway to the village. You had to pass it to get to the rest of the main street. And the owners of the tavern made sure it set the proper tone for the Christmas fairyland.

The tavern was small and looked like a capital letter *A*. It had two porches on its front. One was a small one up top; the other was a longer one along the ground. Mr. Hubert, who had a huge gray handlebar mustache and who worked for the owner of the tavern, outlined the whole building with fairy lights. The porch railings were entwined in lights. Through the windows, more lights peeped out. At night, at Christmastime, Tavern on the Creek looked like a gingerbread house lit by fireflies.

The Lake Shore Road dipped gradually down a slope, into shops and businesses. When you were at the top of this slope looking down the road, you thought you were in the middle of the Milky Way. Fairy lights were wrapped around the old-fashioned street lamps. They spread gracefully over the shrubberies and draped the trees. They were strung around shop windows and doors, and they crisscrossed the street.

The village lampposts were wreathed in evergreen garlands, with fairy lights and big red velvet bows tied under the chins of the lamps. The windows of stores had green wreaths and red velvet bows. The street was as fragrant as a forest.

On Christmas Eve, the people of Homer's Cove gathered around the towering evergreen tree in Veterans Park. Each year, the tree was decorated in lights and on Christmas Eve, they had the official lighting. Everyone sang Christmas songs and then gathered at the firehouse down the road. They drank hot chocolate and ate cookies, homemade by the Homer's Cove Ladies Auxiliary.

"Wrap up well. It's nippy out there," said Harry, when

he came to pick us up. We were to walk together to the tree lighting.

"Is it snowing again?" asked Aunt Sydney.

"Yes, ma'am, it is. A perfect Christmas snow. Light and fluffy."

"Lord! I've never seen so much snow!" exclaimed Aunt Sydney.

"You're in the Adirondacks," said Mr. Platte, coming to the door, tipping his black-and-red plaid wool cap.

"I'll have you know this is not my first Christmas in your precious Adirondacks," snapped Aunt Sydney.

Mr. Platte smiled patiently and helped my aunt into her coat, and her muffler, and her other muffler, and her red wooly shawl.

"You are well wrapped, Sydney," commented Mr. Platte.

"Humpf!" said Aunt Sydney.

Maggie and Harry looked a secret look at each other and giggled.

Amaryllis and I ran ahead to Veterans Park. We tilted our heads back to taste the snow, before the earth did.

"Imagine, Amaryllis, we are the first beings on the entire face of the earth to taste these snowflakes!"

Amaryllis laughed. Out loud. It sounded good.

Maggie called, "Watch the cars, girls. The road is icing up. It's slippery." She and Harry strolled along the snowy sidewalk, holding hands.

Aunt Sydney and Mr. Platte strolled, also. But they were not holding hands.

"Thank goodness for small favors," I whispered to Amaryllis.

"Grinch!" she called me, in a whisper.

The town was gathered about the unlit Christmas tree. All the lights of Homer's Cove were twinkling around us. Through the snow, they became millions of tiny halos. Big snowflakes drifted down from the black sky. They sparkled in the lamplight, as if they were flakes of mica.

Sheila and Ike stood close together at the foot of the tree. Sheila wore a pin that was a Christmas wreath. It blinked red and green, on and off. Ike wore a knit cap with a Santa doll pinned to the front. When he reached up and poked the Santa in the stomach, it laughed, "Ho, Ho, Ho!"

Mrs. Keith had on a cranberry colored cloth coat and Mrs. Francis wore a forest green cloth coat. Both had fur collars pulled up tightly around their necks. They wore stiff felt hats with fur tassels, and each lady wore a holly corsage. They stood with their arms entwined.

"Good evening, girls," Mrs. Keith greeted us.

Mrs. Francis smiled and nodded. Her breath came out in white plumes. Everyone's breath did.

"Merry Christmas Eve, my dears," Mrs. Francis bubbled.

"Mrs. Francis, do you remember the Christmas Eve Mother's Christmas tree fell over and killed the cat?" asked Mrs. Keith.

"Oh, dear, I certainly do!" said Mrs. Francis.

Mrs. Keith looked at Amaryllis and me. "Knocked the cat and impaled it on Mother's knitting needles! Watch where you set your knitting needles! Always!"

"I do think Mother was paying too much attention to the eggnog that evening, Mrs. Keith," said Mrs. Francis to Mrs. Keith.

"I do believe you're right, Mrs. Francis," agreed Mrs. Keith.

Mrs. Mary Murphy marched up through the park in her high-heeled pointy-toed shoes.

Mrs. Francis said, "The poor thing will catch pneumonia in those shoes!"

Mrs. Keith, looking at Mrs. Murphy out of the

corner of her eye, tsked and said, "Tart shoes!"

Mrs. Murphy had a high, pointy hairdo, as if to match her shoes. In her strong Irish brogue, she talked a blue streak to everyone she saw, laughing and flittering her fingers around. Her fingernails were painted bright red, and each one had silver and gold sequins glued on it. She sparkled in the night.

Kee and Laurence came to the tree lighting. Laurence, who was as tall as a basketball player, pulled Kee, who was even shorter than Aunt Sydney, in a child's sled. Everyone they passed laughed and called Merry Christmas to them.

"Too lazy to walk, Kee?" laughed Harry.

Kee laughed back. Her straight black hair hung down her back. Christmas lights reflected in her almond eyes.

Laurence joined in. "Not too lazy . . . too smart!"

"She has you to do all the work, Laurence," said Sheila, laughing.

"Give me a ride next, Laurence!" called Mrs. Murphy.

"You'll poke them spiked heels right through the poor sled," said Cobb.

Miss Marmalyde joined Aunt Sydney and Mr. Platte. She called over to me, "Have you finished *Peggy Lee and the Mysterious Islands* yet, Mack?"

I called back, "It was great! I wish I were Peggy Lee!"

"I thought you would! Merry Christmas!"

"Happy Christmas Eve, Mack," said Shadduck Fey. He had a way of sneaking up on me. He appeared over my shoulder like a dark cloud.

"Yeah. Same to you," I mumbled, begrudging him the greeting and the good wishes.

"Amaryllis, doesn't your sister look exceptionally lovely tonight?" asked Shadduck.

Amaryllis giggled, and ran to stand with Miss Marmalyde.

I, myself, almost puked.

"I have a Christmas present for you," Shadduck whined.

"Who says we're exchanging presents?" I snapped at him.

"Well, it doesn't have to be an exchange. It's a gift from me to you," he whined.

"My mom told me never to accept gifts from strange people," I said.

"But you know me!" exclaimed Shadduck.

"Maybe so, but you're still strange!" I said, and left him.

I walked over to where Poppy and Daisy huddled in

their quilted parkas, fake fur hoods framing their faces and plumes of white breath coming out of their mouths.

"Merry Christmas," I said.

"He's really not so bad, you know," Poppy said.

"What are you talking about?" I asked.

"Shadduck Fey," Daisy answered.

"Good grief!" I exclaimed. "Were you watching? He's such a . . . a . . ."

"A doof?" suggested Poppy.

"Yeah, a real doof. An EWG!"

"What's an EWG?" asked Daisy, wrinkling up her nose in saying the word.

"I made it up. It's spelled E-W-G, and the letters stand for Extremely Weird Group, or in the individual case, Extremely Weird Guy. Or Extremely Weird Girl." Having explored all the variations, I nodded in acceptance of my own genius.

"Wow!" exclaimed Poppy, impressed. "That's good!"

She and Daisy tried out the feel of EWG on their tongues. "EWG! EEEEWWWWG! EEEEEWWWWW-WWWGGGGGGGG!! Wow! Can we use EWG, too?" Poppy asked.

"I guess. Sure. Why not?" I said, actually happy to have two comrades-in-arms in my battle against the EWG.

"You're very clever, Mack," Poppy complimented me.

"Thanks," I said.

"But, you know, Shadduck really can't help what he is."

Daisy chimed in. "Yes! Do you know his father?"

"No. I didn't even know he had one. I had him figured for something that came out of a mad scientist's laboratory."

The sisters giggled and Daisy said, "No. If Shadduck is an EWG, or a doof, it's because his father, and I don't mean to be disrespectful of adults here, but his father is king of all doofs. Know what he did?"

"I'm all ears," I said.

"Well, a couple of summers ago after a softball game down in Lake George Village, everybody went to McDonald's for soda and hamburgers. So everybody in Homer's Cove School and in Lake George School were hanging around the parking lot. Y'know?" Daisy explained.

I nodded. "Yeah, right," I said.

Poppy picked up the explanation. "Well, Shadduck's father insisted on going through the drive-thru, instead of going inside and waiting in line."

"Yeah. Go on," I encouraged her.

"Well, his father goes through the drive-thru, but instead of calling his order into the microphone, he called it into a *GARBAGE CAN*! Can you believe it!" Both girls burst out laughing. Then they both covered their mouths with their hands and arched their eyebrows up high. They scanned the crowd with their eyes, making sure neither Shadduck Fey nor his father were standing around, listening.

"He did what!" I exclaimed.

"Well, he didn't know which the ordering machine was, so he didn't drive his car up far enough. And he called his order out into this garbage can that was right on the side of the driveway. And then, as if that weren't enough when they didn't tell him how much his order came to and everything—y'know how they do?—he called it in again! Twice! And with all the kids standing around, looking and listening."

"Was Shadduck in the car?" I asked.

Both girls nodded extravagantly. Poppy screamed out, "Yup! The FRONT seat!"

"Wow!" I said. I was awestruck by the level of doofism. How does a person ever live down something like that? I was so moved, I actually said, "Poor Shadduck Fey."

Daisy nodded. "Poor Shadduck Fey," she repeated

solemnly. And then we all burst into hysterical laughter, until our bellies felt they'd split and tears rolled down our faces.

Harry escorted Maggie close up to the tree. He looked back, signaling Amaryllis and me to join them. We did, and Maggie put her arm around my shoulders and I put my arm around Amaryllis's shoulders. We were linked like a fence; we were a group.

"Quite a team, aren't we?" asked Harry.

Maggie put her head on his shoulder, in agreement.

"Yes!" agreed Amaryllis.

I heaved a sigh and stared at the stars.

Cobb was in charge of the lighting of the tree. When everyone saw him walk to the back of the tree, where the electricity was, they hushed in anticipation.

Mr. Platte left Aunt Sydney's side and stepped up, underneath the tree.

"You ready, Cobb?"

"Ready!"

Mr. Platte cleared his throat.

"Welcome to our twenty-first annual Christmas Tree Lighting! Homer's Cove welcomes everyone into its embrace on this holy night. We welcome newcomers to our little village, because they bring us new life. We welcome those who've been here for a while, because they keep us on the straight and narrow." People chuckled at that. "And we welcome those who've been here forever. They are our history." People murmured in agreement.

Mr. Platte paused. People surrounding the tree nodded and smiled at each other.

Mr. Platte continued. "We of Homer's Cove are fortunate. Time is different here. We pride ourselves in taking the time to talk to each other. In other places, people never take the time to talk to each other, anymore. Here in Homer's Cove, we do. And we pride ourselves in helping one another. People in other places say, "Every man for himself." Here in Homer's Cove, we say, "All for one and one for all." Here in Homer's Cove, we also mind our own business. There's no idle gossip in Homer's Cove."

Mrs. Francis and Mrs. Keith and Aunt Sydney and Miss Marmalyde looked at each other, smiling and nodding in agreement with Mr. Platte, like happy hens.

"Here in Homer's Cove, we pride ourselves in not worshiping material possessions. There are those in the world who think there's nothing more important than money. They sacrifice time and family for the almighty dollar. Here in Homer's Cove, we take what we need and share the rest. Here in Homer's Cove, it is our friends and families that are all important!"

The group of people clustered under the Homer's Cove Christmas tree huddled more closely together, enjoying the warm spirit of the night.

Mr. Platte finished up. "And so, we of Homer's Cove take the time on this most magical of nights . . . to wish the world a very . . . Merry . . . Christmas!"

The lights of the tree blazed to life. Thirty feet of glowing lights-all the colors of the world-lit the night, as if a rainbow had shattered and fallen to earth in glittering bits, for the sole purpose of lighting Homer's Cove, New York.

People ooohed and aaahed and sang carols and, as one, headed for the firehouse for hot chocolate and cookies.

"Amaryllis, come with me. I have a special plan!" I whispered.

"Maggie?"

"No. No. Just you and me."

Harry saw us head off in another direction.

"Not going to the firehouse?" he called.

"We'll meet you there later," I called back.

"Well, watch the icy roads," he warned us.

"Boy, is he taking over!" I complained to Amaryllis.

"Grinch," she called me again, punching me in the shoulder.

We ran back to the house. We ran to the shed, dragged open the door, and I pulled our old sled out. It hadn't gotten much use over the years. We spent too much time in places that were unfamiliar to us, and we couldn't always locate the good sledding hills. But here in Homer's Cove, I knew the perfect sledding hill.

In preparation for this ride, I'd waxed the runners. They were sharp and they were slippery!

"We're going to have the ride of our lives!" I exclaimed to my sister, leading her up, up Horicon hill.

"But Mr. Platte told you no!" she exclaimed back.

"It will be fine. It'll be perfect!"

We reached the top of the hill, by the boulders. We had a little difficulty getting up there because Trout Creek had overrun onto the road and then turned to ice. But we made it.

Homer's Cove sat in the snowstorm, beneath us. Horicon hill sloped way down, across the Lake Shore Road, down the dirt lane past Sunny's Bait and Tackle, out onto the lake.

I followed Amaryllis's gaze down the hill.

She cried, "But the lake isn't frozen yet! We'll end up in the water! Our bodies will be bobbing up behind Dottie's Restaurant in the spring!"

"No way! I can steer this sled. We can brake anytime we want. C'mon, Amaryllis. We've got so much to celebrate this Christmas. And look around you!" I yelled, throwing my arms open wide, showing her all of the splendor of the most wonderful night of the year.

"Nothing bad can happen on Christmas Eve. We're protected by magic!" I called to the world at the top of my lungs, at the top of Horicon hill.

The road had not yet been plowed of the new snow, and under that was ice. Perfect sledding conditions.

I got on in the front of the sled. Amaryllis climbed on behind me, straddling the sleigh. She tucked her feet in beneath me on both sides. She grasped my shoulders with her mittened hands.

"Ready?" I asked.

She gulped, then said, "Ready."

I revved up the sled by shoving it back and forth in short, jerky movements. Then one big push! We were off!

We went slowly at first. But speed built. Soon we were flying down Horicon hill. Against the night, lights streaked by. The lights of the school—a candle in each window—the lights of houses, the lights of the SugarShack, a blur on both sides of us!

The Lake Shore Road came flying at us!

"Cars!" shouted Amaryllis.

What was traffic doing on the road? Why wasn't everyone at the firehouse?

"Drag your feet! Brake!" I screamed.

But we were moving too fast. We skidded down toward the main road. Our sled turned two complete circles. We screeched! Our sled bumped and was tossed up on its right runner. We leaned to the left. The sled righted itself on both runners . . . close behind a car that sped down the Lake Shore Road. A huge truck barreled down the road, heading directly at us.

Amaryllis squealed and threw her hands over my eyes. I felt the itch and smelled the smell of wet wool.

A thunderous honk blasted out of the truck, but there was no stopping! We flew right in front of the truck! He swerved, we skidded, we were suddenly on the other side of the Lake Shore Road! The blast of the truck horn died with the roar of its engine, as it sped down the road.

We headed straight for the water. The lake flew at us, but I felt no fear! This flight! This speed! The smoothness, the idea of being a razor cutting through the night . . . I was a shooting star!

My heart pounded and swelled, as if it would break through my chest!

I threw back my head and I screamed and hooted with laughter.

I felt Amaryllis tense, then I heard her hoots of laughter join mine.

We soared through the air! To the lake, the frigid waters. And we didn't care! Together, we were invincible!

And then we hit the gravel pile. The sled pounded in headfirst, and the night filled with the sound of screeching steel and splintering wood. The sled flipped up and turned over. It threw me onto the ground, into a mound of snow. It tossed Amaryllis right on top of me.

"Ooooommmmpppphhhh!" she yelled.

"Uuuuuugggggghhhh!" I yelled.

I asked, "Are you all right? Are you all there? Are you missing any parts?"

"All right, all here, all together," panted Amaryllis.

We stood up, rocky from the ride and the spill. We fell into each other's arms and hugged mightily, for the sheer joy of the night and of the flight we had just taken. We shook off the snow and pulled our sled from the snowbank it had sunk itself in. Our sled was twisted and lumped together.

"Our sled looks like it's had the time of its life!" I said.

We staggered home like drunken people, dragging our dilapidated sled and singing "Jingle Bells" and "Holly Jolly Christmas" until our throats were sore.

We hid the sled deep in the darkness of the shed.

"What will we tell Mom about the wrecked sled?" asked Amaryllis.

"We'll come to that bridge when we cross it," I told her.

Chapter 15

"You girls missed the hot chocolate and cookies," Maggie said.

She and Aunt Sydney came home shortly after Amaryllis and I hid the broken sled back in the shed. We had already changed our soaked clothes, and were in the kitchen in our flannel pajamas. Mine had elves; Amaryllis's had angels.

"We're making our own, Maggie. Want some?" I asked.

"No. I had enough. Your cheeks are so rosy, girls!"

I shrugged. "Well, it's Christmas," I said.

"I hope Harry's all right, going all the way down to Lake George Village on a night like this," said Aunt Sydney, tucking her gloves into her coat pockets. She hung all our coats in the closet.

"Well, it's Christmas Eve. He wanted to be with his sister and her family," explained Maggie.

"They should have come up to the tree lighting," I said.

"They usually do. But little Herman, Harry's nephew, has a cold." Maggie kicked off her boots, leaving them in the middle of the living room floor.

"You are as bad as the girls," scolded Aunt Sydney, moving the boots to the closet.

"Harry can handle weather. Harry can handle anything. I'm sure of it," Maggie said in response to Aunt Sydney's scolding about boots in the middle of the floor. But Maggie looked worried. She went to the window, picked up the memory jug, and cradled it in her arms. Her fingers went over it gently, feeling the different things stuck in it, but her eyes peered out the window.

"Snow's falling harder; looks like it has no intention of stopping," she mumbled, more to herself than to any of us.

"White Christmas!" I chirped.

Amaryllis went over to Maggie and rubbed her arm.

"Don't worry, Mom," she said.

"Amaryllis, you're a comfort. I'm so proud of you. Talking and all!" Maggie said. But she still looked worried.

My sister and I sat in front of the TV. *Mr. Magoo's Christmas Carol* was on. We drank down mug after mug of hot chocolate with melting miniature marshmallows. Aunt Sydney served us warm bread pudding with chocolate and almonds. She topped it off with whipped cream. We crammed our mouths, cream and chocolate all over our lips.

"Napkins would be nice," Aunt Sydney *tsked*.

"Why use napkins when we have long sleeves?" I asked, wiping my mouth on my pajama sleeve with elaborate gestures. I even slurped, to punctuate my slobbiness.

"Lord!" said Aunt Sydney.

"Time for bed," said Maggie.

"But, Mom," I whined.

"Your whining reminds me, Mack, what did Shadduck slip into your pocket at the tree lighting? It was something gift-wrapped, I think. I was watching you guys," said Maggie with a grin.

"I didn't even know he slipped anything into my

pocket," I said. "I don't want any Christmas present from Shadduck Fey."

"Now, that's a lovely Christmas spirit," said Aunt Sydney.

I got up and went to the closet. I rummaged around in the pockets. I found the package Shadduck had sneaked in, without my even knowing. The red-and-green Christmas foil wrapping the little box was tattered, and the box was crushed. I opened it up. Inside was a mass of crystal shatters and splinters. I held the open box out, for Maggie to look in.

"Now, there's a mess. What ever happened to it, Mack?" Maggie asked.

I thought quickly. "That's probably how Shadduck Fey gave it to me."

"I don't think so. Sometimes, you can be careless," Maggie said.

She fingered through the shards of glass, piecing things together.

"Look!" she cried, cupping the thing in both hands, holding pieces together. "It was a bird. A Christmas bird!"

It's glass shone in many colors. What used to be its head had a red plume on it. More red plumes looked like its tail.

"What a pity," said Aunt Sydney.

"We'll have a funeral! Right, Amaryllis?" I said.

"I think we can fix it," Amaryllis said.

"I think we can have a funeral," I said

"Tomorrow," said Maggie. "It's too cold and snowy tonight. And, besides, I don't want any talk of funerals." She looked out the window.

Aunt Sydney shepherded us up to bed.

We didn't sleep a wink. Amaryllis chattered away, planning a Christmas morning funeral for Shadduck Fey's Christmas bird that I had killed on our magnificent sleigh ride down Horicon hill.

We were whispering about the presents of Christmases past when I heard Maggie call out.

"Oh!" That was all she said. "Oh!" But I could tell from the way she said it, something terrible had happened.

I jumped out of bed and raced down the stairs. Amaryllis followed.

Maggie was standing with Aunt Sydney. They stood in front of the TV. They had the TV tuned to the Albany station. The picture showed a reporter standing outside in the dark, in the snow. A big road was behind the reporter. Many crashed-up cars and trucks were on the road.

The reporter reported, ". . . and up by the village of Lake George, black ice is the cause of a major pileup. There are reports of serious injuries. Ambulances have arrived at the scene."

"Harry!" Maggie cried.

I knelt in front of the TV screen, my nose pressed against it, scanning the shot behind the reporter. Was Harry there?

"Did you see his truck on TV?" I asked.

"It's so hard to tell. But he was supposed to call when he got to his sister's, and he hasn't called yet," Maggie said. Her voice shook.

"Did you call his sister?" asked Aunt Sydney.

"Yes. No one answers," said Maggie.

"Oh," said Aunt Sydney.

Maggie left the curtains to the front window open. She left the Christmas lights on, inside and outside. We sat in chairs and on the floor, around the room. We looked outside at the snow. We looked at Harry's memory jug.

We waited for the phone to ring.

It didn't.

We waited for the doorbell to ring.

It didn't.

I dozed off and then woke up. I got up and looked at the memory jug, fingering the buttons and the marbles and the eyes.

"This wouldn't be happening if we hadn't gotten involved," I murmured.

"What are you talking about, Mack?" asked Maggie.

"Don't get involved, don't get hurt," I said.

"That's not the way to live," Maggie said.

"Is this the way to live? Always losing someone?" I asked.

Maggie didn't answer me.

Aunt Sydney said, "I think you need to be quiet, Mack. I think you need to go back to bed."

"I'm not going to bed. I'm staying right down here. I'm waiting!" I told her.

"No bed. No bed tonight," said Amaryllis.

I took the memory jug and snuggled with it on the couch. Amaryllis nestled in with me.

Maggie sat in the blue armchair directly across from the front window. She stared out. The antique footstools still surrounded the chair, waiting for Maggie to decide to sell them. Maggie didn't put her feet up on any of them.

Aunt Sydney said, "Well, I'm going to bed. Someone needs to keep her strength up around here."

"I hope we won't need to rely on your strength again, Sydney," said Maggie. Tears glistened in her eyes.

"Oh, my dear, I have a strong feeling that everything will be all right." Aunt Sydney bent down and kissed my mother on the top of her head. "Never fear," she whispered.

Maggie nodded. Aunt Sydney kissed my forehead and my sister's forehead and went off to her bedroom, closing the door behind her.

Maggie jumped up and ordered, "Mack, go get your Special Things Shoe Box. Amaryllis, go get one of those blue Pepto-Bismol bottles. Now, let's see, where did I put that bag of papier-mâché?" Maggie paced the living room, chewing on her thumb, looking in all the nooks and crannies for the bag of papier-mâché.

"What are we going to do, Maggie?" I asked.

"Mack, Amaryllis, we are going to make a memory jug."

My heart leaped into my throat.

"Don't people have to be dead for that?" I asked.

"Not anymore. We are changing the tradition! Besides, it was a southern tradition, making memory jugs for dead people. We are northerners. We are Adirondackers. We are Homer's Covers. Our memory jug tradition will be the opposite. We are going to make a memory jug for the living. We are going to make a memory jug for us! And us includes Harry."

Amaryllis ran to get a blue Pepto-Bismol bottle. I started up the stairs for my Special Things Shoe Box. I stopped and turned.

"What about Dad?" I asked my mom.

Maggie stopped and looked at me. Her face, which had been tense with worry for Harry, softened.

"What about Dad?" she asked me right back.

"My best Special Thing is his medal for bravery," I said.

"Our quiet hero," said Maggie.

"If this is a memory jug for the living, and Dad is dead . . . well . . ."

My mother interrupted me. "Mack," she said, "so long as you keep those memories, your father is alive. I've never pictured him dead! His medal will have the place of honor on our memory jug. I want it that way, you want it that way, and I know Harry would want it that way."

"But, before when I asked you could we make a memory jug, you said no."

"The time was wrong then. The time is right now."

"So, you mean . . ."

"So, I mean, Miss Mack Humbel, go get your Special Things Shoe Box. We are going to make a most beautiful memory jug!"

That Christmas Eve, as we waited for word of Harry, we did make a most beautiful memory jug. It held all the treasures from my shoe box. Amaryllis unearthed three Barbie doll feet, one hand, a tiny Raggedy Ann head, and part of a blue bead baby bracelet she had had when she was a baby. Maggie added a gold locket that her mother had given her and a silver cross Daddy had given her. She put in two charms that looked like tiny baby shoes.

"Your Aunt Sydney gave me one for each of your births," Maggie said. "I've always treasured them."

That night, we built a memory jug. We built it for Maggie and for Amaryllis and for me—our present. For Dad, our past. And for Harry, our future.

Chapter 16

That night, I didn't dream of sugarplums. I dreamed of broken sleds and broken crystal birds and broken cars.

I didn't think I slept at all, but I was asleep when, through my dreams, I heard doors slamming and boots stomping.

I opened my eyes. A dim, snowy light streamed through the window. It was morning, but it wasn't a bright morning lit by sun. It was a white-glowing morning lit by snow. And I wasn't in my bedroom; I was rolled up in a ball on the living room couch. Amaryllis was rolled up next to me.

"Merry Christmas! Merry Christmas, everyone!" boomed a voice. Boomed Harry's voice.

I rubbed my eyes. Was this part of my dream?

I heard Maggie laughing. I heard Aunt Sydney saying, "Coffee? Coffee, anyone?"

"It looks like Santa Claus was here! Anybody hear the sleigh bells? Anyone see any elves? Wake up, you two sleepyheads!" Harry burst with Christmas spirit.

Amaryllis and I jumped up together, and together we ran to Harry, attacking him with as much enthusiasm as if we were Pamela Bowe's attack cats.

Amaryllis was laughing.

I was crying.

"Why, what's wrong, Mackie?"

I sniffled, wiped my nose on my pajama sleeve, and gulped, "Nothing. But you scared us . . . I mean . . . you scared Maggie last night, Harry." I wiped my eyes.

Maggie came over and rested one hand on Harry's shoulder and the other hand on my head. "We were all scared. But I knew he'd be okay. I just knew it."

"I believe I told you so," offered Aunt Sydney, passing coffee out to Maggie and Harry and orange juice to Amaryllis and me.

A cloud shadowed Harry's smile. He told us about his

Christmas Eve. "When your mom called my sister's, we were at church. I missed the pileup on the Northway. Fortunately for everybody, nobody was too badly hurt," he told us.

Aunt Sydney *tsked.* "Those TV reporters. They're always blowing things up out of proportion. Just to upset people. Just to get good ratings! I'm never going to watch the news again."

I laughed. "Aunt Sydney, you're getting more and more like us!"

"Quite a family we are, hey, Mackie?" asked Aunt Sydney, winking at me.

"Yes, quite a family," said Maggie, grasping Harry's hand.

"A family," said Harry.

"Good grief," I said.

I showed Harry the memory jug we'd made the night before.

"It's a Homer's Cove memory jug," I announced.

"What makes it a Homer's Cove memory jug?" asked Harry.

"You don't have to be dead to get it," I explained.

"Thank heavens for that!" said Harry.

"Thank heavens for that!" said Maggie.

"Who wants more coffee?" asked Aunt Sydney, sniffling.

"You crying, Aunt Sydney?" I asked.

"Absolutely not, Miss! You are a thorn in my side, with your nonsense. Drink your juice," she ordered, wiping her red nose on a napkin. "A thorn in my side!"

"We're having a funeral," said Amaryllis.

We told Harry about Shadduck Fey's Christmas bird and its unfortunate demise.

Harry lifted his red baseball cap and scratched the baldness of his head. "First things first," he said.

"Presents?" I asked.

"Boat ride," he answered.

"But it's so cold," complained Aunt Sydney.

"But it's snowing," complained Amaryllis.

"But it's Christmas," countered Harry.

"And it's a tradition," I reminded them.

Maggie had already gone off to round up every coat, glove, scarf, and hat she could find.

"We're so bundled up, the boat might sink!" Aunt Sydney said, laughing.

We walked through the Christmas morning snow, through the glimmering Christmas of Homer's Cove, to the boat dock.

Harry's boat was green. It had red leather seats in it. Harry's boat was an open boat with no roof. The seats were sparkling with newly fallen snow. A wreath of evergreens and red ribbons was tied to the bow of the boat. Red and green and yellow lights blinked on and off, on and off on the wreath. The same kind of lights outlined the entire boat.

Harry's was the Christmas boat.

Lake George was completely still, that Christmas morning. Snow fell gently and silently in soft flakes. There was no wind to blow the snow unkindly into our faces. There was nothing bitter about that day. The snow simply stirred its way down from heaven.

Harry turned the boat on. The engine's roar subsided and blended into the background. It became part of the morning.

We glided, the only thing moving in the world, through the snow. We were warm, nestled in our layers of clothes, nestled in closely with each other. Through the falling snowflakes, colored lights glowed from Christmas trees that people had put on the roofs of their boathouses, and outside on the porches of the homes that lined the shores of the lake.

At some point, Harry was going to get out and water-ski. Maggie was going to drive the boat. Amaryllis and I were going to spot for him. But now, we were just boating through the snow on Christmas Day.

Harry said, "Remember way back, Maggie? Remember that day I found you all, canoeing in the flood in the cellar?"

"Of course, I remember, Harry," said Maggie. She started to sing.

"We were travelin' along, on Moonlight Bay . . ."

Harry joined in. "You could hear the voices singing, they seemed to say . . ."

We all sang, "You have stolen my heart, don't go away, as we sang our old sweet songs on Moonlight Bay."

That was our first Christmas with Harry. That was our first Christmas in Homer's Cove. That was the year we settled down.

Aunt Sydney was very happy.